The Truth About Autumn

A Novel of Suspense

By

Melinda Crocker

Cover art and design: www.jamesfaecke.com

DEDICATION

For my Readers, with gratitude.

ACKNOWLEDGEMENTS

Chris Eanes: editor, publisher, mentor, and coach - and for bringing out the best in me.

Jim Faecke: your work is amazing - thanks for your remarkable paintings for my covers.

Editors and Beta Readers: Katherine, Rita, Sandi & Sharon

And thanks for allowing Sadie, Daisy, & Ollie to spend some time with us. May Sadie and Daisy find each other over the rainbow bridge and be good buddies just like in my fiction.

"Dark Hallways
Have filled my mind
Shadowed thoughts
Are all I find

Traveling down
To a solace so deep
Soothing words
I long to seek

Reaching blindly
I cannot see
Forgotten dreams
To set me free"
-Unknown-

"And there you are.

And here I am.

And no one moves.

And we just stare.

And we just wait

For the other."

-Unknown-

Chapter 1

A mass of cardboard boxes eclipsed the living room wall in the sparsely furnished house. The movers stacked the brown boxes from the largest on the bottom row, to the smallest, which was not much more than a shoebox, on the very top. The items residing in each box was graffitied in big black letters across their front panels. Autumn's eyes swept the script on each box, carefully searching for the one listing items destined for the kitchen junk drawer.

So, this is it, she thought as her eyes skipped over each box. Her entire life compartmentalized into a single wall of cardboard containers and the content details, written in her own handwriting with a bold sharpie marker, mocked her. Not only did it flaunt her slight OCD issue for organization, but it screamed how little she had to show for 32 years of living on the planet.

But maybe that was a good thing; minimalist living was certainly in vogue. *Who knew?* She snorted a laugh. Maybe she was *cool* at last. *Naaaaa*, she thought. Autumn knew she was many things, but she did not believe being *cool* was one of them.

"There," she said when she spotted it. She stood with only the tips of her cowboy boots still on the floor as she reached for the box. It was jammed into the row one down from the top. She eased it out as if she were playing a game of Jenga, which made her laugh aloud when the remaining boxes stayed in place. *I won*, she thought.

Once she had her treasure, she swiveled around and headed for the kitchen as her boot heels clicked on the scuffed hardwood floors.

The floors were wide planked pine and would be gorgeous someday, but in their present state, it was a stretch to see their beauty. Autumn could see it, but she had a good imagination and knew it was going to take a lot of hard work for others to see her vision.

She banged the retrieved box onto the kitchen counter by the deep, old fashioned porcelain sink. She frowned as she noticed the chip missing on the corner of the god awful blue green Formica countertop. The kitchen counter would have to be a priority to replace along with the sink. The once white sink had bold rust stains running from the faucet to the drain hole. She tilted her head to one side and studied it. It looked a little like a wild abstract painting. Autumn laughed. It was her own little Jackson Pollock. The mental list of what she needed to replace was getting longer by the minute.

Autumn's lips pushed against each other in a straight line as she gazed around the kitchen and felt a twinge of doubt. Original plywood cabinets with a slight orange cast to the wood, no cabinet hardware, only faded spots on the old checkered linoleum where the appliances should be, and a strange shade of mustard yellow paint peeling from the kitchen walls. At least there isn't any wallpaper, she thought and laughed again, then shook her head.

What have I gotten myself into?

Her eyes traveled up to the acoustical tile ceiling. It was faded from white to a dingy version of gray and it bumped up against the biggest boxed fluorescent light fixture Autumn had ever seen. The light fixture itself had duel yellowed plastic covers that served as a graveyard for a multitude of moths and other winged creatures.

Autumn closed her eyes and took a deep breath. The smell of dust and decay greeted her nose and she coughed. *Okay, it is a crappy old rundown house, but it is my crappy old house; bought and paid for and I can do anything I want with it. I have no one to answer to—at least not anymore.*

She felt a stinging behind her eyes and turned them to the window above the sink. Her lips softened and began to curl at the edges.

This is my spot. This is my why. She picked this little house on Lake Phillips, North Carolina from some advertisements she received by email. At the time, her life in Nashville was in tatters, and the photos painted tranquility. She felt at home the moment she first viewed the house, and that feeling was still with her.

The lake was framed in the kitchen window like a favorite painting, except this painting was constantly changing. Right now, the sun was descending toward the water and filled the sky with streaks of red and blue before it was reflected in a mirror image on the lake's surface. *Breathtaking.*

The full water view of the lake surprised Autumn each time she saw it. It was visible from here in the kitchen, the dining room, and her bedroom, but the kitchen window framed it so beautifully. After her crazy life in downtown Nashville, this was balm to her soul.

The lakefront water view was the real reason she bought this pig's ear of a house, well, that and the tiny basement burrowed into the hillside that would someday become a recording studio. *The price didn't hurt, either*, she thought with a twist of her lips. Buying the house *as is*, made it possible to pay for it with the equity from her ultra-modern Nashville loft. She managed a full smile. That view was worth some sweat equity. *Damn, it was downright awesome*, she thought.

Autumn shrugged and used a pocket utility knife to cut open the box marked 'kitchen drawer.' As she pulled back the top and removed the brown paper padding, there it was, sitting on the very top of the container of utensils; a bottle opener shaped like a little guitar. Autumn grinned as she ran her hand over the familiar treasure and said, "Come to momma!" It was a gift from a long-time musician mentor who was no longer in the land of the living. It was such a simple piece, but one of Autumn's greatest treasures.

She grabbed a long neck bottle of beer from the ice chest that was sitting where the refrigerator would eventually reside and popped it open, then placed the little metal guitar by the kitchen sink. As the window drew her back once again, she took a swig of her cold brew and felt the icy liquid slide down her throat as she gazed out at her back yard. "My house, my yard, and my damn boxes," she mumbled and then held the bottle up in a silent toast to the view and took another sip.

The view pulled the tension from her shoulders almost as much as the yeasty drink. She was on a finger portion of the large but remote lake. Since the finger she lived on was narrow compared to the rest of the lake, she could view a few houses dotting the woods on the other side, but her house still felt private and isolated.

The gentle slope of the unkept yard was as full of weeds as it was grass, but the yard extended all the way down to the water's edge where a sturdy dock was attached to the bulkhead. The dock had a long ramp that stretched far enough out on the lake that it would be perfect to house the boat she planned on getting one day. If not a motorized boat, she would at least get a kayak or canoe, because Autumn couldn't wait to spend time out on the water.

It was fall, but by next summer, Autumn wanted the yard and dock to get a lot of use. As she gazed at the crop of weeds leading to the water she could picture a groomed lawn in its place. Another sip and she visualized some twinkling lights strung around the deck and could almost hear wind chimes singing in the summer breezes.

At least the dock was new; it was the one feature the real estate agent mentioned at least ten times while taking her on the first viewing of the "fixer-upper." The real estate agent didn't need to sell Autumn on the old house. Despite all the problems, and there were plenty, Autumn fell in love with the place as soon as she saw this view; everything else could be changed.

The day was edging into twilight as a fog moved in across the lake, so Autumn wasn't sure she was seeing correctly as she leaned toward the window, squinted and said, "What the heck?"

Something, or someone, sat at the end of her dock. *Is that an animal or a small child?* Her forehead almost rested against the glass as she gazed at the dark shape. The creature moved and turned so that she could see its head in silhouette. *It's a dog. A very big dog. What is a large dog doing on my dock staring out at the water as if contemplating all the world's problems?*

Autumn put her beer down, grabbed a flashlight from the kitchen drawer box, and headed outside on a wave of curiosity. The screen door slammed shut as she moved from her deck down the wooden steps to the yard. She noticed the animal turn its head briefly toward her at the noise from the door, but then it shifted its gaze back to the water and ignored her. Dusk was speeding toward night, so she flipped on the flashlight and held it toward the ground to keep from tripping on weeds or rocks as she moved down the uneven hill.

Once she reached the edge of the dock the sun all but disappeared, and only a few streaks of pink gave any indication of where it exited the sky. Autumn stopped and flicked the flashlight toward the end of the dock and over the animal's back.

Its fur looked long and sleek, but it seemed to be wet, and to have mud plastered in spots over its yellow coat. *Poor thing*, she thought. She whistled, but the dog continued to ignore her, so she took a step onto the dock. "Here, boy," she said as she took another step, then called, "Are you lost, sweetheart?" The animal kept facing the water but whined loudly and she felt her heart twist. *Maybe its owner fell into the water and needs help?* She eased toward the dog as she tried to keep her cowboy boots from making too much noise on the wood planks as she walked. "It's okay, I won't hurt you," she murmured.

When she was right behind the dog she saw it was wearing a collar and there was a leash attached to it. The leash snaked its way down the dog's side and pooled in a circle on the dock where it was tied to one of the dock's cleats. *No wonder you couldn't come to me,* Autumn thought.

The animal was a rather large female golden retriever. Autumn had one as a child and loved the breed. She eased her hand out and stroked the dogs head. The fur felt like silk and it turned and looked up at her with huge brown eyes as it whined from deep within its throat. She gasped and said, "Oh, my god, what happened to you, sweet thing?" Duct tape was twisted around the dog's mouth. *Duct tape*. She thought as she felt a heat rise from her chest up her neck and onto her face. *Who would do that?* The dog answered with a "ruff" through its cinched jaws and then turned back toward the water.

Autumn's eyes narrowed as she shined the flashlight toward the water. She let the light play over the dark waves as they lapped against the dock with a clapping sound. She let out a breath when she couldn't see anything or anyone but continued to move the light over the water's surface farther out on the lake. Nothing disturbed the inky black water. There were no bodies, abandoned boats, or objects of any kind in the pool of light. The waves were moving as if in the wake of a boat, but as she gazed at the horizon, she couldn't see anything that would have caused the movement.

She thought she heard something above her, but as she turned toward the sound, it was only a bird that darted out of sight into the dark night. She shrugged and looked back at the dog. *Why on earth would anyone do such a thing to an animal?* Autumn felt her face grow hotter and her back stiffen, but she tried to push away her anger as she reached for the leash and untied it. She didn't want the poor thing to think her anger was directed at it.

"Whatever happened to you, we can't fix it here," she said as she turned and began moving toward the yard. She gave a gentle tug at the leash and said, "Come on, let's get you up to the house." To her surprise, the dog moved easily by her side as she guided it up the hill. It stumbled about half way up, but then regained her footing and continued until they were through the deck door.

Once inside, she dropped the leash and flipped on the dining room light. Darkness had fully engulfed the house and the bright overhead light made her flinch. She turned back toward the dog and gasped. Not only was the poor dog muzzled with duct tape, but it was not covered in mud; it was splattered with blood. Dark red blood and there was a lot of it.

Chapter 2

"I understand that, Ma'am, but you have to understand that we don't
have a police policy for locating a dog's owners. For that you will
need to call Animal Control." He looked down at the dog and said,
"I agree that for someone to do this to her is a crime, but
unfortunately, those laws are pretty tame compared to what they
should be, and we would have to have someone to fine."

He was handsome, if you liked the scruffy, haunted look. Autumn
sighed. She had to face it, he was completely her 'type' right down
to wanting to shove him out the door and into the lake. But, not only
was this not the time for an attraction, she came here for isolation,
rest, and to be creative. She took a breath and said between gritted
teeth, "I understood that the first time you said it, but I'm not asking
you to find the owner, I'm asking you to check the blood on her coat.
It isn't *her* blood. I've looked and there are no wounds. She does
appear a little dazed, but I'm not sure if she has been drugged, or is
in shock."

The police officer gazed at the golden retriever, then raised his eyes
back to Autumn. Those eyes screamed he was at least in his 50's, but
his face and body said early 40's. No change in his expression other
than a slight rise of his eyebrows as he asked, "What would you like
me to do? I see the blood and I'll take your word for it that there is
no wound, but what can I do other than observe?"

She placed a fist on either hip and asked, "Can't you at least take a
sample? Isn't there a way of testing if it is animal or human? What if
she was used in dog fighting, or what if it was a person who is hurt,
or even killed?" Autumn glared at him and thought, *I just want you*

to do your damn job, moron.

A small, almost imperceptible curving of his lips. *Damn. Dimples, too,* Autumn thought as his words snapped out at her. "Sorry, but the Lake Phillips police department doesn't have a lab." His smirk said, "Lady, you've been watching too many crime TV shows."

She bent and stroked the dog's head and she turned her eyes to Autumn and whined. She rose and looked at the officer and held out the duct tape she had managed to peel from the dog's mouth and said, "It's getting late and I know you just want to get out of here, but I really feel like something horrible has happened to this dog. If you will simply take a sample of the blood for future reference, and bag this duct tape, you can go, and I'll take it from here."

The policeman opened his metal clipboard without a word and pulled out two plastic evidence bags and a pair of clear plastic gloves, but then, he paused and asked, "Do you have some scissors?"

Autumn handed him the tape, looked pointedly at the cardboard boxes lining the living room wall, then shrugged and turned and headed into the kitchen. She came back with a small paring knife and held it out to him.

"Really?" he said.

Her face darkened as she replied, "It's sharp."

He bent and said, "Easy, sweetheart," then lifted a lock of blood covered fur and cut it off and slipped it into the bag. He handed Autumn the knife and then placed the sealed bag on the clip board. He put the crinkled duct tape in another bag and said, "Anything else?"

"No, you can go now," she said as she gestured toward the front door.

He reached into his pocket and pulled out a card which he handed to her and said, "Here is my card. Feel free to call if anything else comes up." He turned and started toward the door then stopped, swiveled toward her and asked, "Would you like the name of the local vet or Animal Control's number?"

"No, not Animal Control…" a glance at the dog, and then she continued with, "but, I will take the name of the vet. She doesn't have tags, but she may have a chip."

The officer pulled out another card and crossed the room and handed it to her as he said, "The vets, there are two of them, are actually neighbors of yours, and they are quite good. We are lucky to have them in such a small lake community. They take excellent care of my dog, Ollie."

Autumn felt her shoulders relax a little as she thought, *He can't be a total jerk if he has a dog.* She said aloud, "Okay, thanks."

"Not a problem, uh, and welcome to our community," he said as he edged toward the door. At the front door they both stopped and turned as a movement from the corner of the room pulled their attention. Four green eyes in the darkened corner made the police officer jump. "*What tha…*" he said.

Autumn laughed as two identical Siamese cats glided into the light, gazed at him in unison, and then strolled over to the dog and rubbed on either side of her front legs. "Oh, that's Ying and Yang. They like to observe a bit before exposing themselves to new folks." She smiled at the three animals. "They took to the dog right away and she doesn't seem to mind them, either." She looked back at the cop and continued with, "They must think you're okay, too, or they would have jumped up to the very top of the boxes for a more advantageous position."

"Uh, well, okay, good," he said as he pulled the door open and eased through it. "Good luck," he said then pulled the door shut behind himself.

Autumn stared at the closed door then turned to the animals and said, "Okay, that's all we can do for now. Let's hope *jackass* doesn't toss those evidence bags as soon as he gets back to the police station."

She moved toward the dog and said, "Let's get you cleaned up." The dog whined, and the two cats sat close beside her as they stared up at Autumn. "Oh, stop. I'm not going to bath her, which wouldn't kill her no matter what you both think about water, but let's at least get her wiped down enough so we can all get some sleep without dried blood rubbing off on everything."

Autumn looked at the card the policeman handed her, then tucked it into her jeans pocket along with the veterinary clinic card. The cop's name was Dylan McAlister. A very Irish name. She tilted her head and thought, *His accent is not from the south. It's not much of an accent at all, really. Maybe Chicago or somewhere in the Midwest?* She wondered what brought him to North Carolina and how long he lived here. He certainly had a world weary demeaner, so he probably had a lot of baggage.

She shrugged and headed for the boxes to search for the one marked *old towels and rags*. She didn't need any more drama in her life, and here it was showing up on the first night. Blood soaked dog and intriguing law enforcement.

She found the box and pulled it down. As she turned to carry it into the kitchen, she stopped and looked at the animals. They were lying in a straight row watching her. "I can see I'm outnumbered, but don't any of you think that is going to work with me. I'm still the Alpha." She took the box into the kitchen and tore it open as she mumbled, "Yeah, right...you're in for it, Autumn, and you know it." She laughed and added, "You guys I can handle running my life a little, but I need to steer clear of that cute, damaged cop."

Chapter 3

The quaint old downtown of the Lake Phillips community was established sometime in the late 1800's. Most of the buildings were 'shotgun' style, which meant they were narrow on the street front and long from street to alley. Autumn read somewhere that the style was created because taxation was calculated by the amount of street front that was occupied by the building, but she had no idea if that was true.

Autumn chose the North Carolina lake community after she received a series of emails advertising the lake. Next came a tantalizing flyer for her house which had been on the market a while. *Lakefront Bargain*, the reference line read. A little research online about the area and studying real estate photos stimulated the initial trip to check it out in person.

A move based on junk email. She was that desperate for a change. It was only 480 miles from Nashville, but it felt like a different world and had the irresistible benefit of no one knowing her. *Perfect for starting over.*

As she cruised the two-lane main street looking for a parking spot and the Veterinary Clinic, Autumn frowned as doubt welled up and clouded her thoughts. *Did I do the right thing, or will my impulsive behavior get me in trouble again?* Here she was, suddenly living in a rural lake town she knew almost nothing about, with an unknown dog as her passenger, but she smiled as soon as she spotted the clinic. "How charming," she mumbled as she eased past it.

Lake Phillips Veterinary Clinic. It was squeezed into a narrow storefront with a large plate glass window. Autumn continued about a half a block more and found an empty parking spot and pulled her pickup truck into it.

The parking spaces were slanted at an angle instead of the parallel parking she was familiar with, making them easier to maneuver, and each spot was fronted by an old-fashioned looking coin parking meter, much like the old downtown in Nashville. Autumn grinned and reached into her bag searching for change. As she dropped her coins into the side slot of the meter the arrow moved from *time's up* to an hour.

She headed for the passenger side of her truck and tugged at the dog's leash. The golden jumped to the street and Autumn walked her past an old-fashioned diner, several curio and antique shops, and the marquee of a 50's style movie theater that was showing current movies, until they finally reached their destination.

A big yellow tabby cat sat in the plate glass window of the clinic looking out at them. It watched their approach with a slow swivel of its head and a slight twitch of its tail. Autumn gazed back at the unblinking cat before opening the adjacent glass door. "Hope you aren't a runner," she mumbled as she pulled the door open.

Once they were inside, the yellow tabby ignored them and resumed its perusal of the street. Not even a meow to acknowledge their presence. Autumn approached the receptionist, a twenties something blond sitting behind the front counter and said, "Guess we aren't that interesting."

The girl laughed and said, "She's waiting for Doc Terri. Honestly, she's not interested in anyone but her." A glance at her computer screen and she asked, "Can I help you? Are you Autumn Brennan?"

"I am, and thanks for working me in today."

"Oh, no worries. To be honest, we aren't that busy since we are almost into the 'locals only' season."

The girl swiveled around, and Autumn noticed the left side of her hair was shaved and a blue streak snaked its way through a section of her ponytail. Maybe the people who lived here weren't stuck back in another era, only the aesthetics of the town. *Good*, she thought. There were several aspects from that time she did not care to revisit.

"It's usually only hard to get an appointment in the summertime. When the summer people are here we get totally swamped." The girl grinned and handed a clipboard with some documents attached to it to Autumn and said, "Could you fill out some paperwork, please?"

"Sure, but I hope it's only about me, because I don't have any information for this sweet girl," Autumn said as she nodded toward the golden retriever.

The receptionist stood and reached into a big clear glass jar of treats and then offered one to the golden. The dog wagged its bushy tail but gazed up at Autumn before accepting the treat. Autumn laughed said, "Go ahead." The dog jumped up and put its front paws on the edge of the counter and gingerly accepted the morsel.

"Wow, at least we know she is well trained," the receptionist said.

"She sure seems to be. I knew she was easy to lead, but I had no idea about the treat thing. I'm hoping we can get some more information about her today, at least her name, but hopefully who her owner is."

"We will do our best." The girl reached over the counter to Autumn and said, "Hi, I'm Caitlin, by the way, and welcome to Lake Phillips."

Autumn shook her hand and said, "Nice to meet you, Caitlin. Please call me, Autumn." She smiled, then moved over to the leather couch facing the window and sat before she began filling in the paperwork.

The couch was probably once a dark, chocolate brown, but sunlight had faded it to a dusty brown, with gray splotches where numerous derrieres resided over the years. Autumn shifted until she was in the middle of one of the gray patches, and she had to admit, it was quite comfortable. The couch was like a tattered, old pair of slippers that you simply couldn't part with.

Autumn filled out the form and then put her pen down. Caitlin must have been watching, because she immediately stepped out from behind the counter and took her clipboard. "Doc Pat will see you now," the girl said, then turned and led them down a narrow windowless hallway lined with several closed doors. At the end of the hallway she pushed open the last door and said, "Go on in. The doc will be with you soon."

Autumn walked into the examination room, which wasn't much bigger than a large closet. Although it was small, it was comfortably appointed with an exam table, a corner vanity and sink combo, two wooden chairs, and a tiny window looking out onto the alleyway. It was impeccably clean with cheery posters of cute puppies and kittens decorating the walls, and the back of the door held ideal weight charts for both dogs and cats by size.

Just moments after Caitlin left the room and closed the door, Autumn jumped when a sharp rap on the door was followed by the doctor entering the room.

"Hi, I'm Doctor Pat, and you must be Ms. Brennan."

Autumn turned and took the doctor's hand and said, "Please, call me Autumn."

"Well it is good to meet you, Autumn. We have been meaning to come over and introduce ourselves, but we wanted to let you catch your breath first. We live in the house to the left of your property. Since the lots are big in that section, you can barely see the side of our house and deck at this time of year, but once the trees lose most of their leaves, we will be much more visible." Doctor Pat had a voice as smooth and soft as a radio personality and Autumn felt the tension she was holding in her neck and shoulders relax.

The woman was probably in her 60's and medium height with an athletic build. Short gray hair topped her head and round, gold-rimmed glasses covered kind eyes, but those eyes had a twinkle that belied her age. "Oh, so you are my neighbor," Autumn said.

"Yes, myself, and my partner, Terri, and of course, our little dog, Daisy, who really runs the household."

Autumn laughed and said, "Good to know. I haven't met many folks in Lake Phillips, and none of my neighbors." Autumn glanced at the golden retriever and said, "Just my real estate agent and the policeman who came out last night about the dog. He did mention you, and that you might be able to help me locate her owner."

Doctor Pat smiled, nodded and said, "Oh, that must be Dylan. We take care of his dog, Ollie." Then she approached the golden retriever and bent to stroke her head and said, "Did you lose your owner? My, what a beauty you are."

"She was splatted in blood when I found her; that's why I called the police. I didn't find a wound, though, so I assumed something terrible had happened close to her. No blood on her mouth, so I don't believe she bit anything, or anyone, plus, some creep had duct taped her mouth shut." She took a quick breath and continued with, "Your policeman, uh, Dylan, wasn't convinced that it was a person who was hurt, and he could be right. I've heard that people grab dogs as bait for dog fighting, but I did get him to take a sample of the blood before I cleaned her up."

The doctor raised up and her eyes went wide as she said, "Really? How awful…" She looked back down at the dog and frowned as she said, "I don't see any visible damage to her muzzle, but we'll check it more carefully on the exam." She looked back at Autumn and asked, "Did you bath her?" She turned back to the dog and began running her hand through the dog's fur on her neck and chest as she examined her skin.

Autumn said, "No, I was afraid it might freak her out since she had obviously been through a trauma, so I wiped her down with a wet towel as best I could. You can still see some rusty looking spots around her chest area where it was the worst. Oh, and she seemed a little dazed, so she might have been drugged, or it could have been shock." Autumn pointed and said, "See? There and there again on her neck it's still showing."

The doctor nodded and said, "Okay, we will check her blood work to make sure she is okay. If you will just a minute, please, I'll get what I need." She left the room and came back a few minutes later with Caitlin from the front desk. "Caitlin hold the fur up here," she said to the girl as she pointed at a spot, then she removed a Q-tip from a vial and rubbed it on the dog's exposed skin. She held up the Q-tip and the white cotton was now pink. She nodded and said, "Okay, good. Thanks," to the receptionist, then added, "Now, please go get the wand and we'll see if she has a chip." The girl left the room and the doctor placed the Q-tip back into the vial and sealed it, then she took some blood and the dog barely flinched. Doctor Pat looked toward Autumn and said, "We'll test the blood from her fur it to see if it's animal or human, and if it's animal, we will determine what kind."

"Oh, good, thank you. That's what I wanted the police to do, but he kept referring me to animal control." She frowned and said, "Well, he did suggest you."

Doctor Pat smiled, "You'll have to forgive, Dylan. He was a big city cop in Chicago before he moved to our simple little community." She shrugged and added, "He really is a nice man under that grumpy exterior and he is very kind to his dog."

Caitlin returned and handed Doctor Pat the wand, then stood back and watched as she moved it over the back of the dog's neck before she looked at the digital display. "Yes, we have a chip!" She handed it back to Caitlin and said, "Check the database and see if we can get some current information for her."

"That's wonderful! Oh, and can you please inform the police once you get the owner's information? I really want to make sure that wasn't their blood," Autumn said.

The doctor's eyes widened, but she said, "Well, sure---I will do that, and I'll let you know when we have the information on the blood and the results of her bloodwork." She patted the dogs head and said, "Now, shall we give her a more thorough exam, and after that, would you like her to be groomed? We do that in the back."

"Oh, yes, please," Autumn said as she thought, *I am glad this woman is my neighbor and I hope someday I can call her my friend.*

***

Autumn set her purse and keys on the table by the front door. She turned to the dog and said, "Okay, Sadie, let's get that leash off you." The dog wagged her tail and barked, then sat and looked as if she was smiling. Autumn laughed and said, "So, you like being called by your real name?" Autumn bent to remove the leash and placed it next to her purse, then she stood and said, "We'll have to get you a coat for winter and a spot by the door for your stuff." She realized she was already thinking of the dog as hers, but she couldn't help it. Even as she knew it was a temporary situation, she was falling in love with the sweet nature of this animal.

Autumn returned to her car and hauled all the supplies she purchased from the vet's office back into the house. It took several trips. Dog beds, toys, food and water bowls, and a giant bag of dog food. She frowned at the stack of items, but then shrugged. Autumn wasn't sure how long it would take to locate the dog's owner, or if they ever would, but she liked being prepared, and she wanted Sadie to feel at home. What difference did it make if she developed psychological ownership of the dog? It wouldn't hurt anyone but herself, and she enjoyed thinking of Sadie as her own. Besides, she could always donate most of the items if she wasn't destined to stay with her.

"Okay, guys, feeding time," she called as she headed toward the kitchen with the big bag of dog food. They all gathered around her and the cats began their dinner cries as they rubbed against her legs. After distributing food between Sadie's new bowl and putting food for the cats in their bowls, she watched as the dog devoured her food and the cats took dainty bites and she felt a tug on her heart.

They were already becoming a little family and it would be hard to see Sadie go, but still, Autumn hoped the dog's family was alive and well and searching for her. She bit at her lip as she remembered the blood on Sadie's coat and the duct tape around her muzzle. Her imagination turned to the possible causes of such an atrocity and she felt her fists clinch.

If the owner was located, Autumn was going to have to be damn sure that they were not the ones who put the tape on Sadie's mouth. That was simply unacceptable no matter what the circumstances. Her eyes narrowed as she gazed at the dog's silky coat. If she was taken from the owner to use in a dog fighting operation, Autumn was going to make sure whoever did it was prosecuted fully, even if it only meant being vilified in the news. They needed to pay for such horrific behavior.

After the animals were settled Autumn turned to the wall of boxes, sighed and said, "Okay, it's time." But before she could open the first box, Sadie approached the large glass window next to the back door and began barking and growling. Autumn headed for the window and said, "What do you see? Do we have our first wildlife visitor?" She frowned at the view, but instead of a racoon or rabbit, there was a big cardboard box resting close to her back door. *Odd*, she thought.

She opened the door and used one foot to hold the screen door ajar as she reached down and grabbed the box. It wasn't heavy and there was no address label on it, only some brown packing tape holding the lid down. She glanced around the deck and back yard. *Empty*. She heard movement, but as she glanced around all she saw was a big bird as it swept away from the house and behind a tree. She shivered and felt exposed even with no one around, so she brought the box inside and set it in the middle of the floor.

"What have we here?" Autumn mumbled as she walked around the box and examined it. *Maybe a neighbor left it?* It couldn't have been delivered by the post office or a delivery service with no label on it. *Why would they leave it at the back door and not the front?* Autumn wondered. Sadie sniffed at the air around the box, growled, and then edged away from it. Both cats kept their distance, and then jumped up onto the wall of boxes. Once they were at the very top of the stack, they turned to gaze silently at the foreign box.

"Okay, you guys are freaking me out a little." Autumn said, then shrugged, squared her shoulders, and moved forward to rip the tape off the box. "This is ridiculous," she said before she eased the flaps open and looked inside. A large bunch of wildflowers tied with an old blue ribbon took up most of the space, but it was the worn, old teddy bear, with one missing eye that caught her attention. Something about that bear both drew and repelled her. She pushed the top of the box back down and shoved it into an empty corner. "Enough of that!" she said. *Who would have left such a sketchy box?*

Autumn searched her mind for possibilities and came up with one that felt the most comfortable; it was probably some child in the neighborhood simply trying to welcome the new family. The contents were childlike, so it made the most sense. Maybe they were hoping another kid was moving into the neighborhood and they wanted to make friends. *Except, according to the real estate lady, there aren't any close neighbors with kids.*

Autumn shivered again but shook it off as she turned her attention back toward her own wall of boxes. She picked one from the top of the stack and the cats leaped down and raced up the stairs toward the bedrooms. "Cowards," she called after them, then headed toward the kitchen with the box marked *dishes.* She started unpacking plates, but she couldn't stop herself from glancing repeatedly at the mystery box. Sadie was lying several feet away staring at it and every so often she whined deep in her throat.

Autumn rolled her eyes, then stomped over to the unlabeled box, picked it up and headed for the basement stairs. Once in the basement, she shoved the offensive box into a corner, then left the room and shut the door. She could deal with it later.

Some new furniture was supposed to arrive within the next couple of hours and she had to get some of the boxes out of the way. If she didn't clear the space in the living room, she would be stuck with moving the heavy furniture by herself.

Autumn bought the house partially furnished, but the emphasis was on partial, and she was excited to see how her new purchases would warm up the space. The house needed a lot of work, but a good cleaning and some new furniture was the first step, and eventually a lot of DIY. Autumn was ready for the challenge, and maybe, just maybe, in transforming this old house she would transform her life as well, because both needed changes.

As she returned to the kitchen and began putting dishes away again, she paused and glanced into the dining room at the large glass window by the back door. *I better get some curtains after all*, she thought, then returned to her unpacking.

With the lake behind her, she had not wanted to spoil the view and she assumed there would be no one on the water at night, but the thought of being completely exposed after dark was no longer as appealing. She shook her head and dug into the unpacking.

She would not let a lost dog and a strange box become omens. She would not. This was her home now and it had to work. A new start was what she needed, not more drama, because going back to Nashville was not an option.

Chapter 4

Dylan McAlister glanced at the lab report and raised an eyebrow. *Crap. I will have to call her with this*, he thought. Leaning back in his chair he frowned at the white paper and visualized Autumn Brennen's smug expression when he related the findings to her. *Human, female blood, with no match in the system.* It should have taken longer to get the results, but on this report, the one he was hoping would take forever, they weren't busy, so they got it right out. *It figures. My luck in a nutshell.*

After their first meeting, calling her with the lab report results was the last thing he wanted to do. He did not want to be reminded of what a jerk he was, and on top of that, she was right about the blood.

He slid the single sheet of paper into the thin file and put it in his out basket. Maybe he would wait until tomorrow. A glance at his watch. It was late in the day and she was probably busy with her unpacking anyway. With the number of boxes in her living room, she would be at it for a while.

It had not been that long since his move, and although he brought very little with him from Chicago, it still took some time to get settled. Who was he kidding, he still had boxes he dug through when he needed something.

Dylan pushed out of his chair and trudged into the tiny kitchen that served as a break room for the Lake Phillips police department. With only four officers, the chief, and a receptionist to cover their 24/7 shifts; the room was perfectly adequate. Dylan hated it. Compared to the Chicago PD break room, it was tacky, and it reminded him of a

60's television sitcom, right down to the avocado green dining table and chairs. Of course, he had to admit, at least to himself, he pretty much hated everything these days.

With a cup of the thick, black brew in hand, he returned to his desk and pulled out a file on an unsolved string of burglaries going on around the lake. They involved mostly seasonal houses that were empty, but it was only a matter of time until they were going to hit a place with someone at home. It was probably just kids, based on what they were taking, but maybe not, and if they did stumble on a homeowner, kids or not, Dylan didn't want to see what would happen. The owner could get hurt, or since the state was full of proud gun owners, it was more likely some fool kid would wind up in the morgue instead of at his high school prom.

As he was reading over the details of the latest burglary, his thoughts drifted to the red-haired woman that found the lost dog, *Autumn Brennen*. Should he apologize when he first spoke to her, or pretend nothing had happened? When he interviewed her, she was really pissed at him, but fought hard to contain it. A chuckle. He bet she could be a spitfire in an argument.

Dylan shook his head and decided he would be polite and helpful, but not bring up their first meeting. *No reason to try and explain. Why would he want her to know the real reason he was in such a bad mood?* When he got her call, he was ready for his shift to end, and all he really wanted to do at the end of the day, every day, was to bury himself in a bottle of wine or a six-pack, or maybe a combination of both, but instead, he had to take care of her problem. *Not cool and not good police work. At least he wasn't drinking on the job.* A frown as he thought, *At least not yet.*

He bent over the burglary file once again, but before he reached the end of the next paragraph, his thoughts drew him back to the woman with the dog. "Damn!" he said aloud. When the receptionist turned her gray head toward him and peered over her half glasses, he looked back at her and said, "Sorry." Lucy, the receptionist/office manager/dispatcher of the Lake Phillips PD, reminded him of his fourth-grade teacher, Mrs. Cox, and frankly, she scared the crap out of him. He attempted a smile, but it felt stiff, so he ducked his head and swiveled his chair around with his back to her as he stared at the papers in the file.

Why am I thinking about the redhead so much? He rubbed his eyes and tried to focus on the reports. He was prone to overthinking, that much was true, but why so much about this woman? His mouth eased into a deep frown as his brain betrayed him and went back to Autumn Brennan.

She was attractive, but not a raving beauty, and besides, he wasn't looking for someone, even if she was a beauty queen. Her deep red hair was long and wavy, and her green eyes were bright with intelligence, but her petite nose was just a little crooked and her mouth slightly too big to be model perfect, yet her face kept crowding out all other thoughts. Dylan nodded, and a smile tickled at his lips. A real smile. He knew what it was; it was her fierce independence and snarky nature that drew him. *Just like Kate*, he thought, as his smile vanished and was replaced with a deeper scowl.

Each time Kate entered his thoughts, he saw her sweet smile just before a bullet pulled her away. It was much like a movie trailer playing in his head. The trailer always started in the same way; Kate walking around the car reaching for the passenger side door handle, then tossing him the keys as she said, "Okay, Hotshot, you drive." It also ended the same way. Kate grinning at him as the bullet hit her neck and blood spewed from her artery and her lifeless eyes fixed on him as she fell.

Dylan jumped when his cell phone rang, and the image of Kate evaporated. He glanced at the readout but didn't recognize the number, so he grabbed it and growled, "*What?*"

***

Autumn put the last dish away and closed the kitchen cabinet. She turned to look around the room. Empty boxes littered the floor and new dining table. She moved into the living/dining area and turned in a tight circle. With the new furniture and a few personal possessions displayed, it was beginning to look like a real home. Still shabby, but homey. She returned to the kitchen and broke down the remaining empty boxes and then headed down to the basement.

The stairs were steep and narrow, so she was careful to take them one step at a time as she gripped the flattened boxes in both hands. Once in the basement room, she shoved them against a wall and then tugged on the chain of the dangling overhead light bulb. She watched the light swing back and forth from a long rope like cord. It hung from a beam in the center of the ceiling. Primitive, and it worked, but the image was used in one too many horror flicks, so it was one of the first items on her list of improvements. She reached up and stopped the motion. *I bet this isn't even up to code*. She sighed. It was probably true of a lot of the issues in the old lake house. *I must get a good contractor to do an assessment*, she thought. Autumn needed a prioritized list to get started, otherwise, there was so much to do, she might become overwhelmed. Maybe her neighbors, Pat and Terri could recommend someone.

The entire basement consisted of one box-like room. The house was dug into a hillside and the basement was less than half of the main structure's footprint. The room was at least large enough for a laundry nook and some storage. There was a couple of high narrow windows on the lakeside that brought in some light, but it was still dim even at mid-afternoon, so the single bulb helped bring light to the dark corners of the cellar.

Autumn gazed around the room. She planned on eventually covering the plastered concrete block walls with dry wall and adding some soundproofing before she turned it into her music studio. It was too dungeon-like for a den or office, but it would be perfect for recording her songs.

Her musical and recording equipment had already found a home in the room, but most of it was still packed in boxes, and she didn't plan on unpacking any of it, yet-- At least until the room was more hospitable. Except for her guitar. Her guitar went where she did, and right now, it rested against the footboard of her bed.

She wasn't in a hurry to fix the room, even if the record company went away. They were only testing the waters with her, anyway, and Autumn hadn't played a note since her divorce from Richard. She was hoping inspiration would find a home with her here on the lake. *New town. New people. New old house.*

Autumn reached up to turn off the light when she noticed the strange box with no label still resting in the corner. She hesitated. Something about the contents nagged at her, and not in a good way. "Damn," she muttered. As much as she would like to ignore it, she really should throw the flowers out before they rotted. Until she could give it a good cleaning, the room smelled bad enough without rotting flowers adding to the bouquet.

She stood over the box, then nudged the flap open with her boot, but when she gazed inside, it was empty. She jerked upright as her eyes scanned the tiny room then went to the little rectangular windows. Both windows were sealed shut from age and paint. *No one could have gotten in that way.*

Autumn turned back to the empty box. She had no memory of taking anything out of it and that was something she was certain she would have remembered. She backed away from it a couple of steps and then turned to gaze at the staircase. Did the person who left the box enter her house and rescue the contents when she was outside with the delivery men, or when she was at the grocery store?

She frowned and mentally checked off each time she had left the house. She was certain she locked the door every time. Even when she walked Sadie, her old city habits made her lock up and double check it each time.

It could have been a child, she thought, but it gave her no comfort. Someone, anyone, in her home without her knowledge was too creepy to imagine, plus, *how did they get in?* Her thoughts began to spiral until she felt a tension headache coming on. *Why would someone first leave the box, and then return to take the flowers and the old teddy bear?* "What is happening?" Autumn muttered.

Autumn found herself at the top of the basement stairs. She peeked into the empty kitchen, then took a step into the room and paused, but she couldn't hear anyone in the house. Silence resonated through the empty rooms, except for the ticking of the ancient clock still mounted on the kitchen wall.

As she tiptoed into the living/dining room she was greeted by a curious sight. Sadie was sitting at the bottom of the staircase by the front door that lead to the second floor and she was growling. Ying and Yang sat side by side on the new dining room table staring at Sadie like a couple of Egyptian sphinx cats. "Thanks, guys. As if I wasn't already freaked out enough…"

The tiny hairs rose on the back of Autumn's neck, but instead of going for her phone, she stomped across the room and grabbed an iron poker from the fireplace and then moved toward the stairs. "Enough of this crap," she muttered. She would not call the police again, at least not until she knew something more than an empty box or the animals acting weird. "Excuse me officer, I want to report someone breaking in and unpacking a box," she muttered as she glared up the stairs.

Besides, she did not want that damn smart-ass cop to think she was even more of a nut case who needed hand holding to live alone. It would be just her luck that they would send him again if she called it in. Maybe he was being punished for something and they sent him on all the nuisance calls. She could certainly understand him being on the punishment list with his lousy attitude.

Autumn clomped up the staircase making as much noise as she could. She glanced into the first bedroom; it was empty, so she eased down the hallway and past an unoccupied bathroom. When she reached her bedroom, the door was closed. That was how she left it earlier, but she still hesitated. "I'm coming in and I have a weapon," she shouted.

As she edged the door open, she held the iron poker high, but when her eyes swept the room from the closet and bathroom on one side, then across to the sliding glass doors leading to the upstairs deck on the other side, there was no one in the room. She took a step across the threshold and stared through the glass doors to the deck. *Empty.* Autumn lowered the poker, but then gasped and raised it again as she backed up against the wall and stared at her bed.

The dingy worn teddy bear sat on her new white quilted bedspread as it leaned against her new blue pillows with its one good eye staring at her. The flowers were in a vase on the bedside table and daisies were scattered across her bedspread. The blue vase was hers and she had placed it in the kitchen cabinet that very morning.

Autumn bolted from the room, flew down the stairs, and went out the front door. Sadie joined her at the bottom of the stairs and stayed tight on her heels as she moved out of the house, so Autumn slammed the door behind them. At the driveway she stopped and twirled around to look at the house. She felt her stomach tighten and she fought nausea. Her little sanctuary changed in an instant. With a trembling hand she pulled her cell phone from her back pocket and the police officer's card, and then dialed his number. The hell with looking like a nut case. She no longer cared, she just wanted someone here.

Chapter 5

The police cruiser eased down her gravel driveway as it navigated the deep ruts and holes etched by the summer's rain storms. *Another item for the growing list of repairs,* Autumn thought. She tried to manage her frown into a more passive expression as she listened to the crunch of tires displacing the small gray rocks.

Dylan McAlister lumbered out of the cruiser. With the abrupt way he answered her call earlier, she expected him to send someone else to take the report, but here he was one more time. *Guess he drew the short straw again,* Autumn thought as she shifted her weight and pulled Sadie's leash tight against her side. She edged forward a step, but then she managed to stop herself and wait for him to come to her.

As she stood in the driveway her toe began to tap, and as hard as she tried, she could not seem to stop the movement. She had not been back in the house since she made the call, but she managed to edge the door open long enough to grab Sadie's leash and hurry back down the front steps.

The cop moved with the stiffness of a much older man and Autumn absently wondered what that was all about, but then Sadie's tail began a steady thump, and she had to admit, as much as she disliked this man, she was feeling much like Sadie and was glad to see him.

"Afternoon," he said as he nodded and gripped his aluminum storage clipboard to his chest. "First, let me apologize for snapping earlier when I answered the phone. Since it was my cell and I didn't recognize the number, I made the incorrect assumption that you were yet another person trying to sell me something. Now that I have your number in my cell, that won't happen again." He took a quick breath and waited for her response.

Did he just apologize? She leaned back and gazed at him. *Was that a smile he was attempting or a grimace?* Autumn wondered as she shrugged, then said, "No problem, Uh, I've been known to assume something a time or two." She rocked back on her heels which kept her toe from its steady rhythm.

He turned toward her house and his eyes swept from the porch to the second story as he said, "So, do you want to tell me what happened here today?" He turned to her and raised his pen as he poised it above the clipboard. She assumed the paper on it was yet another report. She had not had an occasion to file a police report for her entire life, and here she was with two in as many days. The toe began its rhythm section on the gravel again, so she pushed it slightly behind her and let the foot rest on the toe.

"It's like I told you on the phone; someone has been in my house," she said.

He began to write as he asked, "Did you see someone, or notice anything missing?"

Autumn held Sadie's leash even tighter. The dog gazed up at her as if she sensed the tension, so Autumn relaxed her hold and then she noticed she was still gripping the fireplace poker like a weapon in her other hand. She dropped the sharp end of the poker to the ground and held onto the top as she said, "No—Nothing was taken, and I didn't see anyone, but whoever it was, moved the contents of a box from the basement, to my bedroom and displayed everything on my bed."

Two brown eyes rose from the report and gazed at her as Dylan said, "Moved the contents of a box? Uh, and nothing was taken? Could you have unpacked it and forgot?" He looked back at his report and mumbled, "Moving can be exhausting."

She cleared her throat as she felt her face redden and replied, "No, I'm certain I did not touch that box, and, believe me, there is no way I would have put that stuff on my bed—Or, anywhere near my bedroom."

Eyes glued on the clipboard as he said, "Okay, that's a pretty odd thing for someone to do. What kind of items were placed there." He looked back up at her and she thought she saw curiosity written on his face instead of doubt, but she couldn't be sure.

Autumn moved back a step as she turned to gaze at her second story window. "There is another part to this story." She cleared her throat again. It suddenly felt very dry as she said, "When I got home from the vet's office this morning, there was a box at my back door on the deck. It was a cardboard box with no label and no sign of who left it. It contained some wildflowers tied up with a blue ribbon, a shabby old teddy bear and there wasn't a note on the inside, either. I thought a child must have left it, so I moved it to the basement and forgot about it. The old teddy bear is now on my bed and the flowers are in a vase on the bedside table. It was *my* vase that I placed in a kitchen cabinet just this morning by the way, oh, and there are daisies scattered over my bedspread." Autumn swallowed hard and decided to leave out the part about the animals being more freaked out by the box than she was.

"*Okay*," he said. He drew the word out, and then he looked toward the front door of her house and narrowed his eyes as he said, "Now you have my full attention; that is very strange." He gazed back at her and asked, "You didn't call it in when you got the box?"

Autumn felt her cheeks burn even hotter. "No. Like I said, I assumed it was a child from the neighborhood and that it was harmless. I thought that it might be their way of welcoming the new neighbor." Autumn tapped the poker against her leg and then said, "If I'm being honest, the contents did make me a little uncomfortable for some reason, so that's why I shoved it into a basement corner, but I didn't think it was a police matter. Honestly, I am not in the habit of calling the police. The past couple of days are unusual for me."

He moved toward her house a few steps, then turned and said, "I'm going to check it out and take a few pictures, if that's okay. Do you mind if I collect the displayed items for evidence?"

"No, that would be great." She moved alongside him and added, "I would be happy to never see that stuff again. Do you want me to get the empty box from the basement for you to put the stuff in?"

He shook his head and said, "No, I'll get it. I want to see where they might have been, and I would rather you stay out here until I completely clear the house."

"Well, okay, that's fine. The front door is unlocked," she said.

After he went into the house Autumn sat on the front steps of the porch and Sadie settled in beside her. She absently stroked the animal while she waited. The grooming made the dogs fur even silkier, and she realized that the petting motion was probably more calming for herself than for the dog.

Autumn wasn't worried. She knew the house was empty, and whoever did it was long gone, but when she finally heard the front door opening behind her, she jumped up and swiveled around with her iron poker still clutched in her hand. The policeman's eyes widened, but he moved silently down the steps and put the cardboard box in the back seat of his car, then approached her with his ever-present clipboard. Autumn absently wondered if he slept with that silver metal clipboard. "Well? What do you think, officer McAlister?" she asked.

"Please, call me Dylan. It's a small community and no one here is formal." He looked back at the house and continued with, "No sign of anyone still in the house," he said as he gestured toward the front door. "I think they must have gained entry by the second story deck and through your bedroom's glass doors. They were unlocked and there was a little mud on the deck and railing."

Autumn's head swung around toward the house and she said, "Really? I didn't think to check it after the delivery guys left."

Stupid, she thought, then she said, "I usually check all the windows and doors if someone has been in the house."

"The delivery guys? Any of them seem suspicious or overly attentive?" he asked.

"No, that's a complete dead end. Trust me, they couldn't wait to get through and get out of here and the last thing they were was attentive," she said as she remembered having trouble getting them to listen to her, even about where she wanted the furniture placed. Next time she moved or had furniture delivered, she vowed she would put duct tape on the floor with a photo of each furniture piece. Let them get that wrong. "Besides, I was in the house the whole time they were here. They opened the door for ventilation when they were carting up my new dresser and mattress." She frowned and added in a low voice, "I noticed that they closed it again, but I guess they didn't lock it and I didn't check."

"Oh, okay. Have you been out of the house for an extended period since they left? I mean, long enough for someone to have done this?"

"Yes—I went to the grocery store and I walked Sadie around the neighborhood several times."

He nodded as he made a notation on the form, then said, "You moved here from Nashville?"

"Yes." She tapped the iron poker on the bottom step and looked at him and said, "I'm not usually this jumpy. I lived in downtown Nashville in a loft and I had nighttime gigs all the time," she glanced back at the house and continued with, "but, this really has me spooked."

His eyes rose from the clipboard and flicked over her face until their eyes met. "I don't blame you. That display was very strange and the thought of someone creeping around inside your home would make anyone feel violated." He leaned back and gazed at her as he asked, "So, you're a musician?"

"Yeah, singer, writer, guitar, keyboard, whatever is called for…" she said with a wave of her hand, then continued with, "I am going to make the basement into a recording studio and concentrate more on writing and recording instead of entertaining. It's one of the reasons I moved here and bought this place." *Why did I tell him all that?* Autumn thought as she clinched her jaw muscles and tried to keep from rattling on. She knew she had a bad habit of talking more when she was nervous, and she didn't want this cop to think she was a bundle of nerves, even if that was how she felt.

"Impressive," he said, then his eyes returned to the form and he wrote out a few lines, then he asked, "Do you have anyone from Nashville who might be trying to scare you? Husband, boyfriend, co-worker?"

Here we go, she thought. "No, there isn't anyone in my life who would do this." A sigh, and she said, "It's ex-husband, but don't assume it was him. The divorce is amicable and there is no boyfriend. I'm no longer with a band because it was my exes' group, but nothing there, either, I assure you, so no coworker issues."

"What about your ex? You say 'amicable' but is he the type who might hold a grudge? Or, perhaps he is trying to get you back into his life?" he asked as he raised one eyebrow.

She frowned and said, "No, seriously, I mean it when I say there is nothing there. The divorce was almost too easy. Yes, I initiated it, but there was no resistance on his part." She gazed toward her feet as she added, "I admit he got into drugs, which was one of the many reasons I split from him, but he is much too apathetic to go to this much trouble." She looked back up and could almost feel the disbelief coming from the cop. *Damn, if he fixates on my ex he won't be able to find out who is behind this, because it certainly isn't Richard*, she thought, so she made eye contact and glared at him as she said, "I don't believe he would leave his apartment for long enough to do something this childish, let alone come all the way here to do it. He would consider this type of gesture beneath him." Autumn frowned and leaned against the porch. "I can't think of *anyone* I know who would do this."

Dylan shook his head and said, "Well, that is going to make it more difficult, because in cases like this, it is usually someone who has an unrequited or imaginary romantic interest in the victim, and if its random, they are much harder to find." He glanced up and his eyes roved toward her neighbors on either side before he said, "There have been some small-time burglaries around the lake, but nothing like this. For the most part, I have found this community to be extremely quiet and relatively crime free." A pause, then he added, "At least until now."

Autumn crossed her arms over her chest and said, "What about the dog? Odd that she would show up just before this with blood on her; do you think it could be connected?"

He frowned and said, "I can't think of how that could be, they are such different incidences, but I do need to tell you that the blood on her coat was female, human, and had no match in the system."

She froze, and then said, "*What?* The test already came back? Why didn't you call me or at least lead with that?"

"Yes, sorry. I just got the report this afternoon and I meant to tell you as soon as I arrived, but we became involved with your latest episode." He looked up and sputtered, "I mean, what you called about today. Uh, I just forgot with this new drama---I mean incident."

She noticed his cheeks redden and a bead of sweat on his brow, but she felt no sympathy for his blunder. Autumn's eyes narrowed, and she said, "I asked the vet to call the police department with the owner's information. It showed a woman's name, so It could be her blood."

"Please, don't jump to that conclusion. The blood on her coat could be for a lot of different reasons. I did hear from the vet's office and I let them know the findings on the police report. I also have a call in to the number they gave me for the dog owner, but I haven't gotten a response, at least not yet. I will keep following up, but most likely the two are unrelated and we need to give the owner more than a day to respond. The dog could have been stolen to be used as bait with a dog fighting ring. It's horrible, but it happens, and the blood might be from whoever took her. The attack dog might have bit the handler instead of Sadie, again, it happens. Maybe that's when Sadie made her escape." He tapped his pen against the clipboard and said, "Most of the time I have found this type of incident, I mean the flowers and bear, to be a jilted love interest."

Autumn crossed her arms and took a step forward as she said, "Except Sadie was tied to my dock and I know she is smart, but I don't think she could have done that. So, you've seen something like this with the display before?"

He shrugged and said, "A time or two in Chicago where I worked before Lake Phillips, but it was more just flowers and candy, not creepy old stuff." He tilted his head and added, "I forgot she was tied to the dock."

"And it was always an ex-lover or someone they knew who left the gifts?"

"Well, no," he said as he frowned, and his brow furloughed. He continued with, "Actually, the last one I investigated was the victim's building super and she had no idea he had a crush on her, so she did know him but not well. He had a key to all the apartments, so he was able to let himself in while she was at work and leave her gifts and flowers. She moved, and he was fired, so the problem solved itself. But, the point is that each time I've seen something like this, it was someone who had the twisted thought that they were courting the victim."

She tapped the poker against her leg again and said, "Not this time. I just moved here, so I haven't met anyone, and I am not leaving anyone behind who would go to that much trouble. Please keep following up on Sadie's owner and let me know as soon as you locate her." She turned toward the front door.

He stopped her by saying, "Uh, of course, but I just mentioned it because if it is a stranger, they will be much harder to track down. I'm not saying it will be impossible, just difficult."

She turned and looked at him and said, "So, you said."

He nodded and said, "Oh, okay, just wanted you to know that." His face was bright red as he held up the clipboard and said, "Can you give me your exes name and address just for the report? I'll put a note in your statement that you do not believe it is him, and uh, I need you to sign this report."

"Richard Scott," Autumn sighed and said. He was not going to let it go and she knew Richard had nothing to do with this. She felt deep inside that something else was going on here, but she suspected this man was not going to be of any help until he exhausted the *normal* channels. She looked at him and added, "I took back my maiden name after the divorce." She opened her phone to her contacts list and shoved it toward him so that he could copy Richard's information. As soon as he finished, she signed the form and he handed her a copy. "Thanks," she said, then turned and headed back toward the house with Sadie by her side.

"Okay, please let me know if you see or hear anything else suspicious. Oh, and I locked your bedroom sliding glass door and stuck a piece of wood in the track. The former owner must have left it there for that reason."

"Okay, thanks," she said, then moved up the steps to the porch as she thought, *I must look like a fool not to have checked those locks.*

"You have my number and I don't live that far, so I can get here pretty quickly," he called to her back.

Autumn didn't turn around but waved the hand with the poker in it as she moved through the front door, then closed and locked it. Her face felt flushed and she had a headache starting at the base of her skull.

She wasn't quite sure why she felt so angry toward Dylan McAlister, but she did. Maybe she was only projecting her own fear and frustration about the situation toward him, or the fact that she felt like a fool over the open door, but, she couldn't help but think, *Damn, he pisses me off.*

Chapter 6

Autumn finished washing the last dish and placed it on the drainboard. Her watery reflection floated like a gray ghost in the kitchen window. Night made all the windows mirrors, which reminded her that she needed to get curtains, blinds, or at least some shades for the windows that had nothing covering them. She pulled the plug and watched the suds run down the drain in the sink. She would be happy when her new dishwasher arrived, but for now, she was it.

After she dried her hands, she reached for the overhead kitchen light switch, but her hand froze mid-way and she left the room with the giant fluorescent light still burning. She shrugged and accepted the emotional residual of the incident with the box. *I need the light,* she thought. At least the insect graveyard littering the plastic light cover was gone. She scrubbed and vacuumed the plastic covers until they glistened. They were still a faded yellow, but at least they were clean.

Once she was back in the living room, she turned toward the picture window and she burst out laughing. There was a bright blue king size bed sheet thumb tacked above the glass back door and large picture window. Her temporary solution to the privacy issue. It gave the place a college dorm room look, or at the very least, it had a backwoods hillbilly vibe. She stopped laughing, but a corner of her mouth twitched into a smile. *Tacky? Yes,* she thought, but it did the trick, and to say the cabin was rustic, was beyond being kind anyway, so it fit the space perfectly, at least for now.

Autumn moved over to the fireplace and opened the glass door of the wood stove and tossed a log on the already blazing fire. It was late November and the evenings were getting cold, but she suspected her chill was coming more from within. She shivered as she watched the fire as it flicked and gobbled at the new log. She held her hands out in front of the vents as it shot heat out into the room, but her chill did not dissipate.

The reason for the roaring blaze didn't matter. She loved a good fire and the new wood stove insert in the old fireplace was both safe and burned hot. She turned around and stood with her back to the fireplace and let it warm her before she tested out the new couch. As the heat caressed her back, she began to feel warmer, but as her eyes climbed up the stairs leading to the second story, her shoulders tightened, and her core felt like ice. She mumbled, "Might as well get it over with and then maybe I can get warm."

Autumn headed for the stairs. Luckily, there was a light switch at the bottom of the staircase that connected with the upstairs hallway and she flipped it on. She stood for a moment and gazed up at the light, then turned toward the dog and said, "Want to come up with me, Sadie?" The dog's ears twitched forward at the sound of her name and she edged up from her bed by the fireplace. Ying and Yang were sleeping on either side of the dog's bed, so they moved into her recently vacated space. Autumn trudged up the stairs with Sadie following closely behind her.

Her bed was still neatly made and there was no sign of the flowers or the teddy bear. The cop, Dylan, had even collected all the petals off the quilted bedspread. She sighed and moved past her bed to the sliding glass doors and pulled the curtain closed. She was glad that the former owner had at least left window coverings on the second story. "Wish I had done that before dark," she mumbled to the empty room. She bent and touched the wooden pole in the door track, then rose, unlocked the door and tried to push it open; the pole worked great as a blockade for the door, the cop was right about that. She locked the door again and made sure there was no gap where the curtain met the frame. *Too bad I didn't put the block in earlier today. It would have saved me a lot of grief*, she thought.

Autumn heard something outside the sliders and eased the curtain back and peeked through the crack. A big bird was moving off into the dark and it made Autumn smile. She should pick up some bird feeders and seed to take advantage of all the birds on the lake.

She checked the lock on the door one more time, even though it made her feel a little OCD, then she headed out of the room. Again, she left the lights burning. *Damn the electric bill,* she thought. Autumn stopped abruptly at the bedroom doorway as if she had hit an unseen barrier. She glanced at her feet and they were locked in place. She was frozen and could not move. She could barely breathe and couldn't seem to go forward or retreat into the bedroom.

As Autumn grimaced and closed her eyes the events since she moved into the house flooded into her mind. The joy she felt at arriving and first getting the keys, the disbelief and anger on finding Sadie in such a terrible state, the confusion and anxiety of the box at the back door, and finally the display on her bed, in her space, in her *friggin* sanctuary.

Autumn opened her eyes and let her hands form into fists as she yelled, "*Arrrgh,* Damnit! What the hell is going on here?" Sadie scooted away from the door and headed into the hallway. "Sorry, Sadie," she said in a quieter tone. "It isn't you, sweet girl."

Her space had been invaded, and it made her feel violated. She wanted to put her fist through the wall and burn her bed. What she really wanted was someone to blame, but there was no one, at least not yet, and that was even worse.

She felt a release as hot tears stained her cheeks, and something shifted in her chest, arms and legs. Movement swept through her body and she turned and stomped back to the bed and jerked the quilt and sheets off of it and threw them in a pile on the floor. When she finished stripping the bed, she wadded the bedding into a big ball and carried it downstairs and didn't stop until she was in the basement. There she stuffed everything into the washer, dumped some detergent into it, and turned it on.

Autumn wanted to rid the bedding of anyone else's touch. It might not be logical, but she couldn't stand the thought that some unknown person touched her bed. If she could, she would have thrown it all out, but she didn't have a second bedspread, or another set of sheets. With one quick glance at the empty corner where the box once rested, she left the basement and headed for the ice chest in the kitchen and a cold beer to take to the couch.

The beer helped ease her tension a little, as did an evening of reading, or staring at the fire and thinking while holding her book and trying *not* to think, but at least she felt calmer. Autumn shut the book she was holding, got off the couch and checked the door on the wood stove, then turned off the lights and headed up to bed.

She had already made several trips up and down the stairs to put the clean sheets and quilt on the bed, and after her long day of unpacking and moving furniture, her thighs and calves were burning as she made her last trek up for the night.

Once upstairs she took a hot shower and then, after a slight pause at the edge of the bed, she settled under the covers and propped her book on her stomach to try reading once more. As she snuggled under the clean bedding a faint smell of lemon wafted up. She inhaled the clean scent and it made her smile. *It must be the new dryer sheets. Much better than stale flowers,* she thought, and then grimaced. If she could turn off her thoughts of the past two days, this moment would be just about perfect, but with everything that had happened, her thoughts would not give her peace.

Around midnight, she yawned and put her book on the bedside table. She was having trouble focusing and her eyes kept drooping shut. Although she thought sleep would not come, here she was, propped up in her bed, trying not to doze. She glanced toward the door to the hallway. It was open and only darkness greeted her from the other side. She pushed aside an urge to get up and turn on the hallway lights. She needed to get back to her routine and not let this incident dictate her life.

Sadie was sleeping on her new bed by the door, so she was sure if anyone approached, the dog would make plenty of noise. Her eyes traveled back to her bed where Ying was cuddled at her side and Yang curled around her feet. A perfect night except for the shattered day lingering like a dark thunder cloud in her mind.

Autumn flipped the lamp off and flopped onto her side facing the bedroom door. She had left a single light on in her master bathroom. The door was open a small crack, with just enough light to filter across the floor and keep the door to the hallway slightly illuminated. She wanted to be brave, but she needed at least this small crutch.

She knew her fur alarms would notify her long before someone could enter her space, but she vowed to get a real alarm installed the next day. *Maybe some cameras. Cameras would be good,* was her last thought before the difficult day melted away to sweet, velvety sleep and deep breathing.

Autumn opened her eyes, but somehow, she knew they weren't open. Still, she looked around. It was pitch black dark. The kind of absence of light that obscures all objects. The kind of darkness that doesn't allow even shadowy silhouettes to be exposed. *I left a light on,* was her first thought, followed by, *dream, it's just a dream,* as her dreamworld and reality collided within her mind. She reached out one hand and felt solid wood. *A door?* she wondered, then reached above her head and felt some sort of material. *I'm dreaming,* she thought again, but then she slipped completely into the dream and it became her reality.

She sensed she was not alone in the dark space and could hear heavy breathing to her side. She clutched something to her chest. It was soft and furry. She grinned and thought, *Teddy,* and it gave her comfort.

A small hand slipped into hers from the darkness and she squeezed it. *Who?* Then the door jerked open and light flooded into the space. She was sitting on the floor of a closet in her nightgown and her feet were bare. She gazed at her feet. They were so small, and her toes were tiny. She realized that she was a very young girl again; she was only a toddler. *Odd,* her adult mind thought. The hand she held belonged to a fair-haired boy with gigantic blue eyes. *Brother,* she wondered, but then she frowned as adult Autumn thought, *I don't have a brother.*

"Hey, what have we here?" A voice boomed down from above them.

Her head jerked up at the words and she felt the hand she held tremble and then slip away as the boy inched further back into the closet behind a thick curtain of clothing and coats. She pushed her hair out of her eyes and glared up at the big man.

He stood swaying in the light with a big grin plastered on his face. He was wearing blue boxer shorts and tuffs of sweaty black hair spotted his chest and stood up in small patches on his nearly bald head. He was fat and rolls of pale, bare skin rested in waves just above the boxers. Autumn gazed back down at the black socks on his big feet and almost laughed. He looked like a big clown balloon. The kind you punched and watched it roll almost over then bounce back up.

"What a cutie! Hey, little red, whacha doing hiding in there? What's that you got?" he said in a slurred voice. A big, meaty hand reached down and grasped the teddy bear she was holding by its face.

"No!" she yelled and held on tight. The big hairy man laughed and laughed as her chubby little fingers gripped the bear's arms, and then he stumbled backward with only one button eye from the bear in his hand. He looked at his hand, then down at Autumn and laughed hard enough that she could smell his foul breath.

"Honey come on back. Your time is almost up, so you better make the most of it," a woman's voice called from somewhere beyond the door. *I know that voice,* Autumn thought.

The man looked over his shoulder and said, "Don't be that way—I got some more money to spend and look, I got an eye, and that's gotta be worth something," he said and laughed hysterically as he slammed the door shut.

Pitch darkness again. The strong scent of urine came from the boy still tucked back into a dark corner of the closet. Autumn clutched her teddy and whispered, "I won't let him hurt you." The boy edged forward again, and pity washed over her, but she flushed as she realized she was talking more to the bear than the boy.

Autumn jerked awake and sat straight up drenched in sweat as she gasped for air. Ying leaped from the bed and joined Sadie by the door, but Yang just rolled over and moved away from her feet to the other side of the bed. Autumn was still breathing hard as she said, "What the hell was that about?" She flopped back onto her pillow and thought about the dream. *I don't have a brother and whose voice was that coming from behind the horrible man? It sounded so familiar. Was it a dream or a memory? It couldn't be a memory unless I read it or saw it in some movie...*

It was true that she was adopted, but her parents told her that she was an only child. She only remembered them and had no reason to doubt the information. She never felt the need to pursue her past— not once. *But what a strange dream,* she thought as she shivered. The teddy bear was the same one that was in the box. Same missing eye. *Maybe that's what made me dream it.* Maybe the nightmare was stimulated by finding the teddy bear and her subconscious mind was trying to supply a reason for the missing eye.

She turned on her light and grabbed the glass of water she always kept by her bed. She gulped down half of it, then spent some time doing some deep breathing until she felt her pulse slow down a little. Autumn picked up her book.

Sleep was far away, and she was glad. She did not want to take a chance that she might slip back into that nightmare dream world again. The cause didn't matter; she simply did not want to revisit it. She shivered again and went back to the comforting pages of her book. She wanted the peace of escape instead of searching her confused mind for answers that she didn't have.

***

A light went on in the upstairs bedroom. Rowen pulled his eye from the telescope and glanced at his watch; it was a little after 1:30AM. She must be thinking about him, just like he was thinking about her. Their connection was unmistakable, even after all these years. Too bad she put those tacky covers over her downstairs windows and started closing the ones upstairs. *Oh, well,* he thought. He wanted her to be safe, and anyway, he loved a challenge.

The house he was in was huge and old but met his needs perfectly. It was close enough to keep an eye on her from across the lake and had the benefit of the extra rooms tucked away in the basement where he liked to spend all his time.

Rowen frowned and moved away from the telescope and returned to his laptop. The telescope was old school, but it worked well enough when he needed a quick fix, and in some ways, it was more delicious than the newer technology.

He touched the little arrow to start the video and watched as it played across the screen of his laptop. He smiled as she peeped out of the slider, then pulled the curtain tight shutting out his drone's camera. *Clever girl.* It was almost as if she knew he was watching her, but it wasn't the case, at least not yet. The video was perfect, and it would fit nicely into a montage once he had enough material. He had spent a lot of time editing out any extra footage of the drone's trips across the lake and now the only images were of *her.*

Rowen closed the program and reached out to touch his prize sitting close to the laptop. The drone cost him a small fortune, but what good was it to be rich if you didn't indulge your fantasies? It was built of a new super lightweight technology that made it almost soundless. No alarming whirring sounds when he wanted it to be stealthy.

The drone was made to look like a big black bird. The propeller props were clear and hard to spot unless you were right on top of it. He laughed when he remembered how he told its creator that he was an avid bird watcher when he ordered it. The camera was hidden under the belly of the bird and could photograph from the front or back of the drone. Images could be captured as stills or streaming video. The only thing missing was sound. It couldn't record conversations, but he was working on an idea of how he could add that little extra pleasure. The machine was simply magnificent and worth every penny he paid for it.

He stood and stretched as he thought about the gifts he left for her. The flowers were a nice touch. He knew how much she liked daisies, and she had to be happy to have the bear back. She loved that damn bear more than anything. He grimaced and thought, *Even more than me. Of course, she left the bear behind.*

He rolled his shoulders, shrugged, and sat back down at his laptop and began scouring the four dating sites he had targeted. It took a lot of time to set up his profiles and scroll the sites, but Rowen enjoyed the chase almost as much as obtaining his trophies. Besides, with an IQ of 160 and his double masters from MIT in computer science, it was a piece of cake for him. He really should take the time to create an algorithm to do the search for him, but he grinned and thought, *I do like the personal touch and it's what makes all this so satisfying and fun.*

Rowen scrolled through a barrage of faces. So many lonely women, but none of them lived close enough to be practical. The dating pool in this area was limited, but it was huge around his home in DC. Maybe he should head back to his home base for a while. It would make his search so much easier, but even though he could easily bring his prize back here, which he did several times, he hated to leave *her* for that long now that she was so close.

A face popped up on the screen and he stopped and enlarged it. *Hello.* She was within the fifty-mile radius he set for the local site. She was not a perfect match but very close. Thick ginger hair, a slightly crooked nose, and a soft smile, and from her profile she was a strong, independent woman. *Wonderful!* She was much better than the woman with the dog who was only adequate. She had simpered and cowered and wasn't a challenge in any way. The golden retriever drew him more than the woman. He knew the dog would be a lovely gift. *She* was always crazy about animals and he knew she had a golden as a young girl. He giggled. She used to get so upset when he would hurt some creature when they were little. His fingers flew as he composed his favorite date greeting.

Send.

Done. Time for bed.

Chapter 7

Autumn bolted upright. "What?" she sputtered. A loud banging was coming from her front door. *Is this another dream?* she thought, but then she realized that she was awake and sitting up in her bed. She turned her head and squinted at the clock and it read 11:30AM. She blinked, moved the book that had tumbled to her side, and crawled out from under the quilt.

She sat a moment on the side of the bed as her legs dangled. *How the hell did I sleep so late after such an awful nightmare?* The pounding started again, and she could hear Sadie barking wildly. She ran her fingers through her tangled hair and grabbed the robe she left hanging on the bathroom door and padded down the stairs barefooted.

Sadie was sitting in front of the door staring at it and emitting low growls with an occasional bark thrown in. As Autumn reached the bottom step the dog stood, wagged her tail at her, then barked in earnest again. Autumn patted the dog on the head and said, "It's okay, Sadie," then approached the thick wood barrier and peered through the peephole just as the pounding started again. She jerked her head away, then leaned forward again when it stopped and checked the peephole. "Crap," she muttered, shook her head, then she stood back, took a deep breath and cinched her robe tight around her waist. She jerked the door open as she said, "What?"

He stood in a casual slouch that appeared practiced. Strategically torn blue jeans with a fitted black T-shirt, jean jacket and shaggy brown hair with blond highlights. The hair framed a deadly handsome, although slightly damaged face. *Rockabilly Star wanna be*—her ex, the great, at least in his own mind, Richard Scott. Not the name on his birth certificate, but a name carefully chosen on a drunken night, just before one of their sad little performances, to the amazing crowd of ten, in a just as sad little watering hole.

"Why did you sic the cops on me?" His eyes were bloodshot, and his face was tight with rage. Autumn noticed that his cheeks were just a little puffier than they were when they were together, and there was a hint of scowl lines starting at the corners of his thick lips. She knew he was a few years older than she was, but the life choices he constantly made, or neglected to make, were not without consequence.

"Hello, Richard," she said in a low voice as she crossed her arms over her chest. "What are you talking about?"

He moved his weight from one foot to the next and sputtered, "The damn Irish cop. You know who I'm talking about."

Her head tilted toward her right shoulder and she glared at him. She wondered how many times he had practiced that little speech on his way here as she said, "Actually, I do not."

His eyes rolled toward the sky and both hands flew palms up by his side as he said, "Oh, come on, Rusty, you had to have told him about me."

She leaned forward and spat, "Don't call me that."

"What, *Rusty*? Why?"

That tight passive aggressive smile she knew so well slipped over his mouth. She hated that damn smile. He only pulled it out, along with the nickname, when he wanted to piss her off. Such a coward and a narcissist, she thought. "I did not 'sic' him on you. I told him you didn't have the balls to do it," she said as she leaned against the doorframe. "I also told him our divorce was amicable, but you are making me think I might be a liar."

"He kept me on the phone at least an hour, and then he made me give him my schedule for the past week, like I could remember every little thing I did, and then he even called my landlord to check up on me." His voice rose to a whine at the end of his speech and his shoulders were beginning to droop. He glanced around her at the house, and then at the neighborhood, before his eyes settled back on her and he said, "Why did you move all the way out here to this dump? You had that great loft in town and I heard you had a record company sniffing around." He gazed past her shoulder again as he tried to see inside the house. "And what do you mean, *amicable*? I agreed to everything, even though you were the one who wanted a divorce."

A sigh. No sense in explaining that was the exact definition of *amicable*. She gave up a long time ago on trying to educate Richard, or Dick as she liked to call him, at least in her head. "What are you really doing here, Richard?"

"Can't I check on you? It sounded like you have some troubles and we were married for five years," he said in a soft voice as he gazed at her. He ran his hand through his bangs and cocked his head as he said, "I care about you." No one could switch gears as fast as Richard, especially if he was trying to manipulate you.

Since when? she thought, but said, "Richard, I know you didn't come all this way to check on me. Hell, I don't believe you would have driven across Nashville, much less 480 miles, so out with it, what do you want and why are you here?"

"Uh, well, could I come in? What I want is to talk to my wife," he said.

"No," she said, then added, "I'm not your wife and I haven't been for a while."

"Come on, Autumn, don't be that way," he said as he leaned forward and stuck his hands in his jeans pockets. "Please, I really need to hit the head."

Autumn glared at him, then said, "Okay, you can come in, but you are not staying." She stood back and let him enter.

"Hi, pooch," he said to Sadie, who ignored him as she stared up at Autumn, then he turned to look at the cats who had gathered on the dining room table and said, "I see you still have the evil Satan twins."

Autumn said, "Bathroom is the door to your right. I'm going upstairs and get dressed." When she reached the first step, she turned and said, "Don't touch anything; I'll be right back."

He nodded and scooted into the powder room as she stomped up the stairs to get dressed. When she returned she couldn't see him but could hear him in the kitchen. When she approached the room, she could see him pouring himself a cup of coffee. *So much for not touching anything,* she thought. Richard always created his own rules and did exactly what he felt like doing, so she pointed to the dining room table, and then silently poured herself a cup.

Her eyes felt gritty and her head was starting to pound. She took a deep gulp of coffee and pulled back a corner of the sheet covering the window and gazed out at the water a moment before she turned toward him. He was sitting at the dining room table watching her. He looked at the sheet tacked to the wall and raised an eyebrow and said, "Love what you've done with the place. "

Does the man ever have an original thought? "Not that it is any of your business, but after the incident the officer called you about, I didn't want anyone seeing in at night," she said as she placed her cup on the table opposite him and began to pull the sheets down. "I'm going to get curtains today. Now, Richard, spill, what do you want?"

"Well, first, I admit, I was pissed after the cop called, but then, I got to thinking, you might be in trouble and need a man around for a while to protect you."

Autumn was speechless. She turned to stare at him, then burst out laughing. She simply couldn't stop herself. She laughed so hard she had to bend at the waist to catch her breath. When she was able to stand up straight and the laughter turned into a few chuckles, tears still streamed from her eyes. She wiped her eyes on her sleeves and gazed at her ex-husband and his face was as red as his eyes.

There was a time Autumn would have tried to sooth his fragile ego, but that time was long past, he had seen to that. "Thank you, Richard. I really needed a good laugh. It's been a tough couple of days." She said, then hiccupped, and began folding the sheets before she set them aside.

He sat very still and straight as he gripped his coffee mug until his fingers whitened and he said, "You don't have to be insulting, but then, you always were a ball buster."

Autumn sat at the table and sighed. She placed her hands around the mug and let them warm as she said, "Richard, I don't want to fight, but you can no longer play me. I know all your tricks, and I know you did not fly, or god forbid, drive this far to find out if I am okay. Remember, I am no longer that dewy eyed young girl who is in love with you. I know your concern always lies with you first and the rest of the world later." She took a sip of coffee and leaned back as she said, "What is it? You can't pay your rent without my steady income? Your dealer needs a payment? What?"

His eyes narrowed, and his lips adjusted into a straight line as he leaned forward and said, "You really think that little of me? We were so good together. You are the only one I ever really loved."

Autumn turned and looked out at the lake, then back at this man that she had once adored, and she realized she felt nothing for him, not even pity. "Richard, I know you think you loved me, but that wasn't love, that was the desire for adoration, and ultimately, convenience. I'm sorry, but I honestly think you are incapable of love. We are divorced. I do not love you. I do not hate you. I nothing you."

He pounded a fist on the table and started to surge out of his chair, but then settled back down and stared at her. His face went from tight anger, to a relaxed half grin, then he said, "Okay, okay, I guess

I deserved that, but you always could call me on my bullshit, at least, after we were married a while; that was one of the things I liked about you…" He shrugged and said, "Yes, I did get kicked out of my digs. It was right before the cop called. And, yes, my dealer wants some bucks on my tab, but nothing serious, he knows I'm good for it."

"If you needed money, why not call me instead of spending the money to come all the way here with this stupid story?"

"The boys and I have a gig about 20 miles from here, and they booked a bunch more through North and South Carolina. I thought I could earn some bread and come see what you are up to at the same time. I really do miss you, and, they wanted me to tell you there is always room for you onstage, if you are interested."

And there it is. The record deal he must have heard about, she thought. A small smile, before Autumn said, "I wouldn't mind seeing the boys, but I do not want to play with your guys again. I don't like sliding backwards once I have taken a step forward." She took another sip of coffee and then said, "There is a possibility for a recording contract, but they want me as a single, and only if they like the new songs, once I get them written that is…"

He shrugged, "I know that about you not looking backwards, and truth, I admire it. I always seem to be sliding backwards, but that's what drugs and booze are for, they help with the lies we tell ourselves."

Autumn's eyes widened. This raw honesty was rare with her ex. Maybe her leaving him was as good for him as it was for her. She said, "I hope you are able to one day live without that crutch, or at least not give yourself to it entirely."

He nodded and said, "Yeah, I hear you and I'm working on it. The gig isn't until tomorrow, so can I crash here tonight? I can sleep on the couch—uh, unless you have other arrangements in mind." The half-lidded look and sly smile appeared again. Autumn knew he would never change, and he would only be able to momentarily disguise his manipulative nature.

She rose from the table and padded over to her purse and pulled out her wallet. She had gone to the bank before the furniture delivery came and withdrew a considerable amount of cash to make sure she had enough money for tips and miscellaneous household supplies. She returned and handed a wad of bills to him and said, "You can't stay here; it just won't work. I have too much going on right now, but there is a clean little motel at the edge of town and it won't be booked up at this time of year. It's pretty cheap, too."

He stood, stuffed the money into his jeans pocket, and moved forward to hug her. She stiffened, but then allowed it for a moment before she pushed him away. "Okay, you better get going, I've got a lot to do today."

The easy, cocky grin returned as he said, "Okay, cool, maybe you can come and see us tomorrow night. I'll text you the address. Take it easy, girl." He headed for the door and turned just before he left and said, "Good to see you and I really hope all this works out for you and you get that record deal."

She followed him and said, "Take care, Richard." Then she pushed the door closed behind him and turned the dead bolt.

***

"What is he doing there?" Rowen mumbled as he watched the streaming feed. He hovered the drone just beyond the trees, but then chanced moving it closer to the window. He could clearly see she was upset, and then her ex-husband slammed his fist onto the table. Rowen almost ran from the room to his boat, but instead, he gripped the controls and held the drone steady as he continued watching the silent drama as it played out in front of him. His shoulders relaxed along with her face as he watched them ease into what looked like a conversation instead of an argument. Then a curious thing happened, she got up and retrieved some money from her purse and gave it to him. "Why, would you do that? He doesn't deserve it—He took enough from you when you were married to that loser," he said, and then moaned. Why would she give him anything but a boot out of the door after the way he treated her?

Rowen knew all about her idiot ex-husband. He couldn't believe his eyes as the scumbag got up and hugged her, *hugged her*, then practically skipped to the front door. When she headed up the stairs and out of sight, he moved the drone to the front of her house and got a good look at the rental car and its license plate as it pulled out of her driveway.

Rowen brought the drone home and picked it up. He entered the house through the basement walkout and placed it on the table before he moved to the large dining room wall just off the common area.

The wall was a magnificent shrine to her. It held all the pictures he had taken and the ones he pulled from the internet as he pieced together her life since she left him behind. He had almost no pictures of them together when they were small, so he contented himself with seeing pictures of her and her new family.

He shook his head and frowned. His mother was never into taking pictures of her children. She was too busy screwing any man who she could squeeze some money from. Two faded old pictures of when they were toddlers was all he had, and he doubted it was mom who took them. But there were lots of pictures of the girl who became Autumn to her foster parents. The same foster parents became her adoptive parents, so he never saw her again after their mother took her out one day and came back alone.

For years he was terrified she had killed her and he did his best to stay quiet and out of her way, so she wouldn't do the same to him. He learned very early how to be invisible. He considered it one of his super powers. It was years later that he learned the truth and how she was the lucky one.

Rowen moved closer and examined the photos. His eyes lingered on several and he reached out and touched them lightly. When her adoptive parents joined Facebook, they began posting every highlight of her life. On her 30th birthday they posted a whole montage of her from childhood to adult. When Rowen found their account, he couldn't believe the treasure trove of photographs he could access. His eyes swept over her years from childhood to adulthood.

Her experiences were much different than his. He lingered over her graduation picture. It was the one in which she looked so much like their mother. He didn't like that one. Too bad her adoptive parents were both dead; they were a terrific source of information. There was very little Rowen didn't know about her, though. Between social networking and the necessary posting for her public presence, her whole life was out there for him to live with her.

Rowen moved to the section of the wall that contained her ex-husband and drew a big red X through his face. It felt so good that he did the same thing to every picture he had of the man, then he ripped them from the wall and tore them into little pieces. That felt even more satisfying.

He headed to the bedroom and slipped into his 'going out' clothes. Black sweat pants, black tee shirt, black hoodie sweatshirt and a black baseball cap over his short cropped blond hair. He grabbed his 'go' bag and checked it. Everything was there: duct tape, extra-large plastic bags, generic rope, a taser, and large hunting knife. "All set," he said as he moved toward the door. *Time to go hunting.*

Chapter 8

"Come on, man. What are you waiting for?"

"Okay, okay, Josh, I'm coming," Timmy said as he trudged down the grassy slope beside the big old white house.

Everyone knew the house and used it as a landmark for directions. It was constructed long before Lake Phillips became a town, or the lake was developed. The family who built the elaborate Victorian owned the lake and sold it to developers when the younger generation hit hard times, at least that was what Josh's mom said, and he couldn't wait to see what treasures were hidden inside.

It was a cloudy night and not even the moon was free to help guide them. Timmy slipped and placed his hand on the side of the house to keep from sliding the rest of the way down the hill. "I need some light. Why can't I turn on my flashlight?"

"Don't you dare turn on that flashlight before we get into the house. You know how visible a light is from across the lake—Are you *trying* to get us caught?" Josh shook his head and thought, *Stupid.*

"No, but if I fall and break a leg we will get caught anyway when you have to call an ambulance," Timmy mumbled.

Josh kept silent and continued down the hill as he thought, *It would serve you right if I just took off and left you,* but he immediately squashed the thought; he would never leave Timmy behind, especially with a broken leg. He slowed down so that Timmy could follow him as he guided his steps down the hill.

The two had been best friends since kindergarten and Josh was always looking out for Timmy, except that one time, and that was big enough to make taking care of Timmy a lifetime chore he freely accepted. The guy saved his life. Big, dumb Timmy had saved him.

It was when Josh fell off the old barn. It was the summer between their 3rd and 4th grades. They loved that old abandoned barn with its weathered gray siding, open hay loft, crumbling stalls, and the smell of hay still lingering in the air. Their best games of cowboys, pirates and even super heroes were played there.

The day Josh died started with a rousing game of chase that wove through the dimly lit barn and ended up in the hay loft. One minute he was laughing and holding onto the side of the big open window of the second story, and the next moment he was flying in a downward spiral while still holding onto the rotten board as he watched Timmy's face frozen in horror in the loft. For a moment it was exhilarating, but then he hit the ground, and everything went blank.

Timmy told him later that he went down fast, hit the ground with a big whoosh in a cloud of dust, and then he tumbled down the hill and landed in the pond face down in the muddy water. Timmy had raced down the old ladder, ran to the pond, and fished him out, and then pounded on his chest until Josh sputtered water and started breathing again. He was a goner, but Timmy brought him back, and he would be forever grateful.

They never did tell their folks about the incident, or they would have forbidden them from playing in their favorite spot, well, at least Timmy's folks would have. Josh's dad was long gone, and his mom never knew where he was most of the time--and she was too busy to care. It was okay. His relationship with his mom existed in a mutually comfortable *don't ask, don't tell*, so, Timmy's heroism went unheralded, but from then on, Josh felt as if Timmy was his responsibility. He owed him his life.

The house was in total darkness as expected. Josh's mom was the local real estate agent and she loved to talk about her work. Josh only half listened, until he heard her going on about listing vacant houses, and that was when the idea struck him, and he started paying attention. He knew instantly that what she was prattling on about could be a gold mine.

She told him that she charged the owners of the unoccupied houses extra to take care of their places. Josh had smirked and kept listening. *Taking care* meant his mom would call someone to mow or clean, and then charge the owners even more for the service. Not only was she cleaning up, *literally*, with the service, but it also made it easier for her to sell their places. His mom loved listing houses that were summer houses, unoccupied and fully furnished. What Josh heard was 'empty houses full of stuff to steal and sell on eBay.'

The boys worked through her list all summer and now that it was fall, they almost had enough money for the new X-box they were going to keep in Josh's basement. *Man, it was going to be a great winter of gaming.* They might even have to ditch school more than they did now. They were both *latch key* kids, and Josh was good at forging his mom's and Timmy's parent's signatures. He grinned in the dark and quickened his steps again. For once, Josh didn't mind it when the summer ended.

When they reached the back of the house Josh headed around and through a covered porch, pulled out the key he swiped from his mom's files, and opened the basement door. "A covered patio outside of the walkout basement with a nice deck above it overlooking the lake," is how his mom's ad read. Josh had thought, *Good cover for sneaking into the empty house.*

Once inside, they left the lights off. Although the house was surrounded by woods, they didn't want anyone from across the lake to notice a light in the empty house. They were on a finger channel of the lake, so it was close enough for houses on the opposite shore to see across and notice.

Josh pulled the curtains closed and they both turned on their high-powered flashlights and flicked them around the basement room. They were in a large well-appointed great room with couches and chairs and a dining room table sat to the back and side of the big room. They separated and began scouting without a word. They had been friends so long that they understood each other without saying much. Something that came in handy with all the thefts they committed around the lake this summer.

Josh's flashlight settled on a telescope, "Hey, check this out," he said as he moved toward it. The front of the scope was wedged through a gap in the curtain. He gazed through the lens and was looking at the old cabin directly across the lake. That new lady from Nashville had bought it through his mom. He smiled when he remembered his mom talking about how happy she was to unload the dump.

He turned to look for Timmy and said, "Hey, whoever was using this thing; he wasn't gazing at stars. What a perv..." He laughed, then spotted Timmy across the room with his flashlight trained on something on the other side of the dining room table and he said, "What are you doing, man?"

"You got to see this, Josh."

Josh crossed the room and stood beside his friend as he shined his flashlight on the wall as well. Splashed over the entire wall was a strange assortment of photographs of various sizes. The small hairs on the back of his neck stood on end as the bizarre collection was flooded with light from both of their flashlights. It both drew and repelled him, and he felt his feet edge closer as he examined the pictures.

A lot of the photos seemed to be of the same woman, but, and this was strange, at different ages. You could tell it was her even though in some of the photos she was younger than his mom but older than Sally, his neighbor that he had a secret crush on, and with others, she was just a little kid. "Weird," Josh mumbled.

But, then it got weirder, not that it wasn't already spooky to have dozens of photographs of the same woman taped to the wall. At the bottom of the collection there was a separate section set apart from the other pictures. Here, the pictures were surrounded by a faded blue ribbon—almost like they were framed. Josh froze in place but found himself bending at the waist to get an even closer look. Sweat broke out on his forehead and trickled down his back.

The framed pictures weren't just set apart by the ribbon, they were different. It wasn't more pictures of the same woman, but it was several women who looked a lot like her. They had similar hair and body type, but instead of clear digital photos, they were pictures from an old-timey camera. These looked grainy and had a white border around each one. Josh saw something like it on the internet once and they called them "Instamatic photographs." The women in the pictures were all sitting or lying in different positions and they were wearing strange clothing, kind of hippie like—*Maybe from the 70's?* Josh thought. A lot of the women were crying and a couple of them were either asleep, or worse.

Josh felt his stomach tighten and he leaned forward and squinted at the last photograph. He bolted upright and turned his light around the darkened room. The image of the woman danced before him as he headed for the door. She was lying in a pool of dark liquid and what looked like blood oozed from several areas of her body. "Let's get out of here," he called over his shoulder through tightened lips.

"Yep," Timmy said. "Right behind you."

As Josh reached the door he pulled it open and gulped fresh air and then turned toward his friend and said, "Come on, Timmy."

Timmy was standing still instead of following Josh. His flashlight was spotlighting something. Josh took a step toward him and said, "We need to go," but as he got closer he saw it was something so strange he froze. It was a drone that looked like a big black bird.

Timmy said, "Cool," and then moved closer toward it and his light flashed over a laptop on the desk beside the odd drone. He added, "Don't you want to get the telescope or the laptop? And, look at this cool bird drone."

"No, don't touch that stuff," Josh snapped and moved back to the door and as he slipped outside and flicked off his flashlight he said, "Let's go, Timmy--Right now!" Then he added in a tight whisper, "Come on, or I swear to god I will leave you here alone."

Timmy nodded and followed him without another word.

***

"What is taking so long?" Richard grumbled, then he moved from the curtained window to the tiny bathroom to splash water on his face. As he rose from the sink the image gazing at him from the mirror was one that he knew intimately; every feature, every pore, both the flaws and the perfections. It was an image he had loved and hated his entire life. Image was *everything* in Richard's world, and no matter how many times he felt like he reached a pinnacle, he would find a new flaw that sent him crashing down.

He ran a finger over his right cheekbone and down the side of his sculpted jaw. You could barely see the tiny scar from the 'freshening' he got from a top Nashville plastic surgeon. Autumn thought all the money he siphoned off their joint account, and then from her secret account, which wasn't so easy to find, was strictly for drugs, booze, and gambling, but nope, most of it went for his image.

As he pulled his hand away from his face he noticed a tremor run through his fingers, so he placed both hands together and headed for his duffle bag. He pulled out a small bottle of bourbon and took a swig. He felt the burn ride down his throat and then took another drink.

Richard sat on the edge of the bed as he waited for the bourbon to work its magic and turned his gaze around the room. Autumn was right, it was clean, but she hadn't mentioned how tiny and shabby it was. He smirked. She probably enjoyed thinking of him sinking so low, but then, that dump she was living in wasn't any better. *What was she thinking? Why give up such a fabulous loft in a town where music was everything and move to this Podunk place in the middle of nowhere?*

The day was a hard one and he needed his guy to get here. Lake Phillips was such a crappy little nothing town. He had to reach out to his bandmates to find someone for his connection. Richard had drug connections all over the south, but they were in real towns, not nowhere hick towns like this one. His gaze turned back to the window and he took another drink.

He hated seeing Autumn today. Back when Richard first met her, she was barely beyond her teens. He still remembered how starry eyed and naive she was. He loved viewing himself in her eyes. Those shinny mirrors said he was a god, so he married her to keep the image going both to himself, and everyone they met. Now, he could hardly stand to be in the same room with her and couldn't believe what he saw in those same green orbs. *Pity, shame, disgust? Whatever*---he thought and then shrugged.

She said she felt nothing for him. *How could she feel that way when her love for me was so great?* But the truth was in her eyes and she meant what she said. The unpardonable sin was that she laughed at him. She not only laughed, she had damn near collapsed with her fit of amusement. His cheeks burned as he remembered it and he took another long draw on the bottle. *Whatever*, he thought again as he shrugged. *At least she gave me the money.*

Richard grimaced when he remembered what he said to her. He had almost choked on the words about the booze and drugs hiding the lies he told himself, but he knew she had to hear something like that to loosen her grubby fingers on her money. He saw some guy say the same words to a girl in a movie. Autumn was so *friggin* tight with a buck. That wasn't always the case. In the beginning, she spoiled him with clothes and equipment. He liked the old Autumn, the new one, not so much.

He smiled and thought about Candy. She was waiting for him back in Nashville. Okay, she wasn't Autumn, but she looked at him like Autumn once did. She was just a waitress in a diner, and he was moving into her trailer instead of nicer digs like Autumn's loft, but that would change. He knew she had the potential to be a real moneymaker after he softened her up a bit. She had big blue eyes and big boobs and not a lot going on upstairs. He had taken her to a club at the edge of town a couple of times, and Buck, the manager, was eager to have her as one of his dancers. The girls made big tips if they knew how to be extra friendly and he could see Candy playing the part with expertise. *Yep, the future is bright, so the hell with Autumn,* he thought. *I've still got what it takes.*

He heard a light tap on the door and jumped up from the bed. As he jerked the door open he said, "Finally!"

The man standing in front of him was tall and thin, with short cropped blond hair. He was dressed in black and was carrying a bag in one hand, but he had a childlike face. *Small time drug kingpin,* Richard thought as he chuckled and said, "Come in, Man, I've been waiting for much too long, buddy."

"Me too, but I needed to wait until it was dark," the man said. He reached into the bag and pulled out a large taser gun. As Richard opened his mouth to shout, a wire exploded from the taser and hit him in the chest. He felt an electric shock radiate from his chest to the rest of his body. His muscles tightened, and then seized before he collapsed to the floor as a roaring in his head and ears obliterated everything else.

Chapter 9

A persistent knocking woke Autumn from a deep sleep. Her first thought made her smile, *I can't remember any bad dreams.* But, with the second barrage of knocking she sat up and moaned aloud, "What, now?" Then she swung her legs over the side of the bed and said much louder, "Richard again? *Why?"*

She grabbed her iPad from the bedside table and opened it to the app of her newly installed outdoor cameras. Her eyes widened. Instead of Richard standing at her front door it was not only the cop, Dylan McAlister, but he was with two other officers. The eldest of the group was wearing a baseball cap that had 'Chief LPPD' on it. She frowned and swallowed hard. *What has happened? Did they find Sadie's owner and she is dead?*

Autumn jumped up and slipped into jeans and a shirt and padded down the stairs barefooted. At the front door she keyed in the new alarm code and pulled the door open. As her eyes flicked from one serious face to another she repeated her thought aloud, "What has happened?"

"Hello, Ms. Brennan. I'm Harold West, the chief of police for Lake Phillips. May we come in?" the elder policeman said as he ignored her question. He was a large man, probably in his late fifties, with the girth of someone who worked out his entire life, then suddenly stopped, but kept eating as if he was hitting the gym every day. Heavy muscles were obscured by fat.

She stepped aside and motioned them in. The chief moved through the door with the ease and confidence of someone in charge despite his size. Dylan followed with a tight nod as he passed her, and finally, a female officer marched by who was short and slender. The woman's eyes flicked over her and then darted around her front room. She had the look of an eager puppy ready to take on the pack.

Once inside, they followed Autumn to the dining room table by the large window and she said, "Please, sit." The chief and Dylan sat at one end of the table, but the female officer stood behind her chief with her hands on her utility belt.

Autumn opened the curtains. She purchased and installed them while the alarm company was installing her new system the previous day. *Maybe that's why I didn't have any nightmares*, she thought. She was very glad she had replaced the sheet covering before this group got here, especially before the female cop with the nervous eyes saw it. She bet the woman would have profiled her into a class dominating the wrong side of her jail bars.

The morning sun streamed in and almost blinded her, so Autumn moved to the other end of the table and shifted her chair so that the sun was behind her and sat. She swallowed hard and wished she had some coffee as her eyes slid from one face to the other, but all three were void of expression, even jittery eyes. She wanted to ask if they would like coffee as an excuse to guzzle some, but her legs felt like they might betray her if she moved to do even the simplest task, so she clasped her hands on the table and waited for them to speak.

"Miss, Brennan, I believe you have met my officer, Dylan McAlister, and this is another of my officers, Judy Wilson."

Autumn nodded at them and said, "Has something happened? Did you find Sadie's owner? Is she okay?"

Chief West's eyebrows rose, then he shook his head and asked, "Sadie? Who is Sadie?"

Autumn turned to gaze at the dog who approached when she heard her name. The golden sat at Autumn's side and she stroked the dogs head before she turned back toward the group. Her eyes went from person to person, but Dylan wouldn't make eye contact with her, and the other two just stared. Autumn frowned and said, "This is Sadie, she is the dog I found on my dock with blood on her."

The chief leaned back and shifted his weight on the wooden chair and said, "Uh, no, we aren't here about the dog." The female cop's expression changed from bland to what Autumn decided was a smirk as the chief leaned forward again and asked, "Ms. Brennan, when did you last see your ex-husband, Richard Scott?"

Autumn's head snapped up and she said, "Richard? Yesterday, uh, yesterday morning. Why?" Her eyes narrowed as she shifted her gaze to Dylan and then she asked, "What has he done, now?"

Dylan kept quiet and examined his hands, but the girl cop smiled and nodded her head in a *I knew it* demeanor. Autumn tilted her head and gazed at each of them again, but this time she settled on the chief as she waited for an answer. Anger slipped into a cold knot in her stomach. *Did Richard get into a drunken brawl or use the money I gave him to buy drugs?* But then she felt a little light headed. *Did something happen to him? Did he finally kill himself getting behind the wheel when he was blitzed out of his mind on drugs I financed? Or worse, did he hurt someone else when he was wasted? Why the hell did I give him money?*

"Why did he come to see you?" The chief asked.

"What?" she mumbled as she felt her face burn. She took a breath and blurted, "He said it was because he was upset Dylan, uh officer McAlister, called him about someone breaking into my house, but, he finally admitted he has a gig close to here with his band." She looked at each of them again, then dropped her eyes and said in a low voice, "And, the usual, he wanted money."

The chief sat up straighter and asked, "Did he do that often? Ask for money? Did that make you angry?"

"What? Uh, yeah, he came to me a few times begging for funds after we split up. I usually don't indulge him, but this time I did give him some." She sighed, and her cheeks burned hotter as she continued with, "I get a little exasperated with him, but I don't think it makes me angry---I would say sad and disappointed instead of angry." Her eyes narrowed, and she said, "Look, I don't want to be rude, this is my new community and I want to fit in and be cooperative, but why are you asking me all these questions? What difference could it make to the Lake Phillips police department if I give my ex-husband money? Even if he did something illegal with the funds, why are you asking me about this when you should be asking him." She leaned back in her chair and her lips formed a straight line as a slow burn started in her neck and spread up to her cheeks. *Stay cool*, she thought as the anger continued to replace the embarrassment she initially felt.

The chief rubbed one of his hands over his face and he said, "I'm sorry to meet you this way, Ms. Brennan, but these questions are necessary." He sat up very straight and tilted his head to one side as he said, "I am very sorry to inform you that Richard Scott was found dead early this morning in the Lake Phillips Motel."

"*What?*" Autumn whispered as she leaned forward and gripped the edge of the table. She felt the heat dissipate and it was replaced with a chill as her core felt like ice. "What did you say?" She repeated a little louder, but her voice sounded hoarse.

"Wilson, get Ms. Brennan some water." The chief barked. The female officer scooted into the kitchen then a glass of water appeared on the table in front of Autumn.

Autumn clutched the glass and gulped half of it down, then gazed at them and asked, "How?" She sighed and said, "He has had a drug problem for years, and I have expected this, but it's still a shock."

"Not drugs," Dylan said. He was finally looking at her and his eyes brimmed with concern.

The chief turned to him and gave a small shake of his head, then turned back to her and said, "His death was not from a drug overdose, Ms. Brennan, I'm afraid he was murdered."

"Murdered? Are you sure? He has threatened suicide in the past, but I never thought he really meant it," Autumn said.

"If you could commit suicide by stabbing yourself 14 times while tied to a chair, that *would* be something," officer Wilson mumbled, then barked a small laugh that she tried to turn into a cough.

The chief turned and gave her a withering stare, then turned back to Autumn and said, "Sorry about that, Ms. Brennan. Officer Wilson is new and shouldn't have said that." Wilson turned a bright red and froze in place. The chief continued with, "No, ma'am, we are certain it was murder, there can be no question. The doc described it as overkill and personal. Uh, do you know anyone who might have done this?"

Autumn whispered, "*What?*" But she couldn't hear what he said next because her ears were ringing too loud to hear anything else. The vise that was forming around the top of her head squeezed and she saw Dylan spring toward her as the world went from gray to black.

***

Autumn glanced at her watch and frowned. The police left hours ago, and it was still early afternoon, but she wasn't quite sure what to do to pass the time until she could go to bed. That was all she really wanted to do; crawl into bed and pull the covers over her head, but she knew she wouldn't sleep and she didn't want to be alone with her thoughts, or worse, dreams.

She paced the room and found herself at the plate glass window in the dining room. It was a beautiful fall day. The sun was bright in an almost cloudless blue sky. Tiny ripples danced across the lakes surface until a family of swans drifted by and disrupted them as they created their own wake. A squirrel scampered up a tree, then sat and preened himself as he stared back at her. She leaned against the windowpane and wished she could cry. *Why can't I cry?* she thought.

After the police left she thought the tears would come, but they didn't. She was horrified Richard had died in such a grisly manor and she couldn't believe she would never see him again, but otherwise, she felt numb. *What is that about? The man was once the love of my life and all I feel is numb?*

Autumn turned and moved to the couch and flopped down. *Why was Dylan McAlister so distant? He wouldn't even make eye contact with me.* She realized he owed her nothing including a *heads up,* but come on, he could have at least acknowledged they had met, and the Chief acted as if he knew nothing about Sadie. *Did he throw the report about the dog away?* she thought and then grabbed a pillow and held it against her chest as she gazed around the room.

She had just walked Sadie. All the boxes were unpacked. The house was relatively clean, and she didn't feel like doing a deep cleaning dive. She didn't feel like doing anything really. She noticed the local paper lying by the couch, so she leaned over and picked it up.

Autumn rarely read newspapers. She liked to get her news on the internet or record the news on TV and fast forward through the parts she didn't want to see, which was most of it lately, but the newspaper was complementary for new homeowners, so why not check out the local scoop. As she flipped through the pages an ad jumped out at her for a kayak sale at the local hardware store. It looked like a mom and pop store and it had several models she was interested in. She jumped up from the couch, grabbed her keys, turned to Sadie and said, "Want to go for a ride?" The dog barked and headed for the door. Autumn snapped on her leash and followed her out. A little retail therapy might help her feel better.

On the ride to the store she let Sadie put her head out of the passenger side window and they both enjoyed the fall weather. She tried not to think about Richard, but images kept flooding through her mind. Not just images of their time together, but of what must have happened to him. The girl cop said he was stabbed 14 times. *14 times…*She shook her head and tried to clear that image from her imagination. *Overkill and personal. It must be about drugs,* she thought. She always knew drugs would get him in the end, but not like this; she never imagined something like this. "What did you get yourself into, Richard?" she mumbled.

A nagging feeling that she was missing something and that his death was somehow connected to the blood on Sadie kept creeping into her thoughts, but she pushed it away. *That is impossible, simply impossible*, she thought as she couldn't imagine a scenario where the two incidences would fit together. Autumn shook her head and concentrated on the road, but her thoughts kept going back to what had happened. She didn't believe in coincidences and there were so many strange things happening since she moved to Lake Phillips.

Autumn pulled her truck into the parking lot of the hardware store and saw wheelbarrows, grills, camping gear and finally kayaks displayed in the front of the store with a big "Fall Sale" banner hanging from the porch roof. She got out and told Sadie to stay in the car as she walked through the merchandise.

A salesman approached her in front of the kayaks and she told him she wanted the 10' blue sit-on-top, then followed him into the store to complete the purchase. He was so happy with the quick sale he threw in a paddle and life vest, and then helped her load everything in the back of her pickup truck. I love mom and pops stores, she thought as she backed out of the parking lot.

She drove home and unloaded the kayak, then drug it down the grassy hill to her dock where she turned it upside down. She took the rest of the equipment into the house along with Sadie, then went to get a beer as she looked through the window at her new prize. That big bird was hovering on the other side of the trees again, but when she went out on the deck to get a better look, it swooped off over the lake. *I should have gotten some bird food and a feeder at the hardware store,* she thought. "Next time," she said, and then went back into the house.

Autumn stood at the kitchen window and stared out at the lake. She absently picked up the little guitar beer opener and flipped it around in her hand, then hung it on the cup hook she had placed beside the window. It was the perfect home for it. As she looked at the little guitar she had a sudden urge to play her guitar, so she went up to the bedroom and picked it up.

She hadn't played in a while, and it was months since she had the urge to write, but suddenly the notes and words were tumbling out of her. She grabbed her notebook and began to scribble as she played and sang. The song was about love and loss, and she knew it was her coping mechanism, but was grateful for the release. Her cheeks felt wet as the tears began to flow and then turned into hacking sobs. Finally, despite the choking sobs, she felt as if she could breathe again.

Chapter 10

Autumn's eyes flew open and she glanced at her phone as it chirped from her bedside table and thought, *Is it morning? I know I just closed my eyes.* The last thing she remembered was thinking that she would never go to sleep, but that was around midnight, and as she squinted at her watch, it read 10AM, so she must have slept soundly for about 10 hours.

She sat up and fumbled with the phone, but then she recognized the caller ID and smiled, so she swiped to answer it as she said, "Hello?" Autumn cringed as she realized how much her voice sounded like a croak.

"Hi, Autumn."

Autumn's shoulders relaxed when she heard the voice floating through her cell phone. This was not the first time the vet called her to check up on Sadie. *No wonder she is such a great veterinarian,* Autumn thought. Doc Pat's voice always sounded so full of compassion; the woman had the ability to calm both her animal patients and their caretakers with a few simple words.

It was a shame she wasn't the one who told Autumn that Richard was brutally murdered. Maybe then she wouldn't have fainted in front of most of the Lake Phillips police department. "Hi, Pat," she said as she remembered the vet asked her to drop the doctor title, then she cleared her throat and continued with, "Oh, sorry, but I'm not at my best right now."

"That's why I'm calling. I hope you don't mind, and I don't want to intrude, but Dylan called us to let us know, and Terri and I were wondering if there is anything we can do?"

"Oh," Autumn said. She tried to rack her brain with what phrase she should follow up with. She first thought of the lie most people use after a loss, *Oh, nothing, I'm fine.* She could tell the truth, *No worries, he was my ex, and although I once thought he was the sun, moon, and stars, I was really disappointed in him, so I should feel nothing now, but I still feel like crap and can't stop thinking about how he died.* She left it with the single word and hoped this kind woman would understand.

"The last thing you probably want is this old lady poking her nose into your grief, but Dylan was concerned about leaving you alone. I sense that you are a strong woman, and I am sure you can handle this, but I still wanted you to know we are here if you would like company."

Dylan was concerned? He sure didn't act like it. Autumn thought but smiled as her eyes stung with tears. Pat seemed to read her so well and they had only just met. She must be an expert in the empathy department. "Thank you, Pat. It is nice to know you guys are right next door and I can't tell you how much this call means to me, but I really am okay."

"Look, we have office hours until around 2:00, then we will be home for the weekend. So, please, come and have drinks and dinner with us tonight."

"That is very sweet, but my ex, Richard, was in a band, and they were my band also for a while, anyway, they called me last night and they're doing a little tribute for him tonight. I was thinking of going, although I really don't feel much like it. Uh, and I don't know what the place they are performing in is like, so it could be a little sketchy." Autumn squeezed her eyes closed and thought, *I am rambling. Why do I always ramble when I am struggling with emotion?*

"Really? Where are they doing it?"

"A place called, *Cowboys*? I think it is in the next town?" Autumn said.

"Cowboys? Oh, yes, we know it well. It isn't far from Lake Phillips. You can't exactly call it a town, though. It's a couple of establishments, but they are more like a pit stop before you get to a real town. It has a gas station, the bar with a restaurant, and even a post office." She chuckled and said, "They are all named Cowboys, Cowboys bar, Cowboys Post Office, you get the idea---The bar is a good place for some great unknown musicians to strut their stuff, and the crowd is mostly harmless locals, so it's not scary at all."

"Uh, oh, okay, good to know." Autumn hesitated, then took a quick breath and blurted, "Would you guys like to go with me?"

"I'll ask Terri, but I am sure she will jump at the chance. I'm the homebody, but she drags me out sometimes because she loves music and dancing."

"That would be great. I think they are starting around 9:00," Autumn said, then added, "but, I will confirm the time."

"Okay, we could pick you up at 7:00 and have dinner first if you like. You can discover some of our local cuisine." She laughed, then said, "All joking aside, the food around here is quite good if you like Southern cooking."

"I do, and that would be lovely, and, thanks, Pat."

"It will be our pleasure---See you tonight, and Autumn, please call if you need anything," Pat said.

"Will do, and thanks, again," Autumn said.

After she disconnected, she gazed at the guitar sitting at the end of her bed. Before last night, it rested untouched against the footboard since moving day. She tilted her head and sighed. If she were honest, she had not written anything substantial for months. Now, it was like a damn had broken. She hadn't even had her coffee, but she felt an overwhelming desire to play it. She shook her head and wished tragedy wasn't the reason for breaking her hiatus, but she was still grateful it allowed her to release some of her pent-up emotions.

Autumn crawled across the bed and picked the guitar up and caressed the smooth wood, then dropped her legs over the side of the bed and began strumming. She sang the early songs she had written for a man that she had created in her head; a man who was flesh and blood, but still imagined. Then she sang the song she wrote last night for the real man, the flawed man, the man who she had loved and lost long before he met such a grizzly end to his life. She mourned both what could have been, and what really was, and somehow, she again found some comfort in another session of tears and song.

"Enough," Autumn said as she put down the guitar and headed for the bathroom to shower. She had to find a place somewhere between anger and sadness so that she could put Richard to rest.

***

When they pulled into the bar's parking lot after dinner, Autumn was very glad she was with Pat and Terri, otherwise, she probably would have turned around and headed home. The lot was filled with pickup trucks, oversized SUV's, and motorcycles, a lot of motorcycles. The half-lit neon sign spelled *Cowb,* instead of *Cowboys.* It looked like the interior would be loud and crowded and that was the last thing she wanted to experience right now.

The entrance was located on the side of the windowless building. It was dark and dingy with a few empty beer bottles scattered around an overfilled trash can by the door. Autumn could hear the thump, thump sound of loud music reverberating from the wood plank walls. She sighed as they got closer, but Pat reached out and patted her on the shoulder as Terri lead the way to the door.

The bar had all the earmarks of a rough hangout. She played in plenty of similar bars in Nashville, but they were familiar to her, and after all the strange things that happened recently, she was on edge and cautious, but if Pat and Terri felt comfortable coming here, she was sure it couldn't be too bad.

As they moved up the stairs to the front entrance the smell of hamburgers and fries wafted out along with some jukebox version of Pink singing "Disconnected." Autumn smiled and thought, *Okay, this might be a little different than I expected.* "Maybe we should have eaten here," she said to the couple.

"They actually do have really good food, but it is just hamburgers, fries, and typical bar food," Terri replied as they pushed through the front door.

"Hey, Marty," Pat called to the man behind the bar as they walked in. He waved at her and winked. He looked like the guy who played Phil Dunphy on Modern Family, and not like he would be tending bar in a place called Cowboys that had Pink as one of the recordings on the jukebox. *A working jukebox is unusual enough, but the contradictions seem to just keep on coming,* thought Autumn.

Autumn gazed around the dimly lit room at the people eating, drinking, and dancing on the miniscule dance floor. There were Gen X'ers hanging out with Baby Boomers, and some motorcyclists in full gear sitting at the bar and playing pool in an alcove fitted with two pool tables. She nodded and thought, *I think I'm going to like this place. It's different. Both happening and homey. Must be a small-town thing. Everyone coming together.*

Terri headed straight for the dance floor greeting people with hugs as she went. Pat grinned and led Autumn to a table close to the back of the room where the band was setting up. "It's fun, right?" she said. The crowd looked more like a local town hall meeting than bar crowd, that is if participants could drink and dance at meetings.

"Yes, and not what I expected," Autumn said. The guys in the band waved at Autumn and then each came over and hugged her. She introduced them to Pat and then they returned to the stage to finish their setup. Just as Terri returned from the dance floor, Autumn turned to look at the bar and she spotted Dylan McAlister sitting on a barstool staring at her. Her mouth sagged, and he shrugged and waved. She found her hand rising in a return wave.

"Should we ask him over?" Pat asked.

Autumn looked at her and stiffened, then said, "I guess so." It felt as if everything began to move in slow-motion. Pat raised her arm to signal to him and he rose from the barstool and made his way through the crowd until he was standing in front of them with a long neck beer in his hand. *Why did I say I guess so? Why didn't I say no?* Autumn thought. Somehow his presence made her feel the full weight of everything that had happened from finding Sadie to Richard's death. *Face it, Brennan, not death, but murder*, she thought as her shoulders sagged.

"Can I buy you ladies a round?" Dylan asked.

"Sure," Terri said.

"Want to join us?" Pat added.

He looked at Autumn and she slowly nodded her head. She knew it wasn't his fault, and she didn't want to feel such animosity toward him, so she attempted a smile. He grinned and waved to their waiter and then sat between Autumn and Pat. After they ordered their drinks he turned to her and said, "Sorry about this morning, but it wasn't my rodeo and I was told to keep my mouth shut before we came."

Autumn looked at him for a moment. No smile or twinkle in his eye, and he appeared to be completely serious. She accepted her beer from the returning waiter and took a sip before she managed to say, "Sokay." She turned to look at the band who was starting to tune up their instruments as she thought, *Sokay? Who says that?*

A light touch on her arm, then Dylan said in a low voice only she could hear, "I know we got off on the wrong foot at our first meeting, and I'm sorry I didn't take you seriously, but I just wanted you to know, that's because of my issues, not yours. I know things didn't go well at our second meeting, either, but I was really trying to help you out and I honestly didn't mean to offend you."

Autumn turned to gaze at him and remembered Pat's words about him having a history. Maybe he wasn't as much of an ass as she had made him out to be in her mind. She nodded and said, "Okay, why don't we let it go? Circumstances have been out of the ordinary since I got here, and it may have colored my view a bit, so it's possible I over reacted a little."

"No, I was a jerk, but maybe not as much of one as you thought," he said, then the band started playing and all conversation stopped unless it was in a shout. Autumn smiled and reached out her hand. Dylan took her hand and they shook as he smiled back at her, and then they both took a sip of their beers as they turned to watch the musicians play.

Autumn listened to the familiar music and felt something she had not felt in a while; nostalgic. She had some good memories from being on stages with the band and Richard, but she realized she seemed to only allow the bad memories in. Maybe it was safe to feel all of it now that Richard was gone. Every past has both good and bad if you are secure enough to see and feel it.

The band played a few songs, then Mikey, the lead singer, stepped up to the microphone and said, "Tonight we are doing a tribute for one of our family that we lost last night. This song is one he wrote with his wife, Autumn, who is in the audience." He turned to look directly at her and said, "Autumn, could you please come up and join us for this one song?" She stiffened, and he held out his guitar and everyone turned to look at her and applauded.

"Shit," she mumbled as she felt her legs go weak.

She had said it so low only Dylan heard, so he leaned forward and said, "You don't have to do it."

Ambushed. She nodded at Dylan and got up and walked to the stage. With each step her legs felt a little stronger. She would do this for

Richard. Not the tarnished Richard she had come to know so well, but the early Richard. The one who had made her feel special and given her the confidence to take to the stage.

Mikey reached down to help her up and she glared at him and he winked. She found herself placing a kiss on his cheek and then she took his guitar and moved around to face the crowd. A glance back at Mikey, and then Autumn said, "Richard was actually my ex-husband, but we had a very special relationship for a very long time, especially musically. It's been a while since I sang this song, so be patient with me, folks," she said.

As the words started flowing from her lips and her fingers eased over the familiar chords, she slipped back in time to a place where pure love had created the melody. It didn't matter if it was a love she built on a fantasy; it was still love. When she finished, hers were not the only cheeks that glistened with tears. She gazed at her table and Pat, Terri, and Dylan were all smiling at her, then they stood and continued applauding.

The rest of the seated people in the room stood in unison and she felt a bubble rise in her chest. She swiped at her tears, then her eyes paused on one of the faces in the back of the room. The man was tall with short blond hair, and he had intense blue eyes that she could see even at a distance. She felt a chill as if she knew him, but couldn't remember from where, and then he slipped out of the front door, so she shook it off and turned and nodded at Mikey. He took his guitar back and helped her down from the stage and she headed straight for the ladies' room to pull herself together as the blue-eyed man was quickly forgotten.

When she came out of the ladies' room Dylan was waiting for her in the tiny darkened hallway. They were alone, and as she stood next to him, the unique smell of an old bar began to close in on her. The air was heavy with stale cigarette smoke and spilled drinks. Autumn wondered if the smells would ever dissipate, even with years of not allowing smoking.

As she glanced around she spotted a back door, and then Dylan said,

"Want to get some air?"

Autumn wordlessly shook her head yes, and he led the way to the door. Once outside, they perched on a small wooden deck with stairs that descended to the alley. She leaned against the deck railing and gulped in the cool fall night air but then coughed; the air was tinged with the smell of an overflowing dumpster just below them. She leaned over the rail and gazed down. The open dumpster had mounds of black plastic bags flowing over the sides and onto the ground. Two skinny dogs tore at an open bag, then grabbed a half-eaten burger and ran down the alley.

"Poor things," Autumn whispered, then turned back toward Dylan and said, "Thanks for coming to check on me. I was a little shaky after that song. Lots of memories."

Dylan nodded and said, "Understandable. You sang beautifully, though. I am not sure I could have done that. I mean, go on stage like that after what happened, not sing; I know I can't sing."

She laughed and said, "Thanks." She gazed up at the night sky and added, "It wasn't easy, but it actually helps me to sing. Musicians can get a lot of emotion out with their music."

"A good ability to have. Unfortunately, this cop doesn't have any way to release tension. Maybe I need to take up a hobby." A sad smile, then he leaned against the back of the building and said, "By the way, I still haven't gotten a call back from Sadie's owner, Jan Miller. Tomorrow is my day off and I plan on driving over and see if she is home, or if her neighbors know where she is."

Autumn's head snapped back toward him and she said, "Can I go with you?"

A frown, then he said, "*Uh,* no."

"Why? You said you are going on your day off."

"You still can't go with me. I may not want to do it on official time, but only because the chief wouldn't approve of that kind of follow up for a dog, but that doesn't mean a civilian can go along with me."

"Why?" She smiled and asked, "Do you think Sadie's owner is dangerous?"

He laughed, "No."

"Then, why?" She crossed her arms over her chest and looked him in the eyes and asked, "Am I a suspect?"

He blushed deeply enough for her to see even in the dim lighting. He cleared his throat and said, "Not for me."

"Your chief and that woman cop?"

"Look, you argued with Richard the day of his death, you have a history, and who else knew he was in town? It would be crazy not to have you on the short list."

She tilted her head to one side and her eyes narrowed as she said, "Then why don't you suspect me?"

He looked at her and said, "Instincts." He continued to hold eye contact as he expanded with, "I've been doing this a long time and I have a pretty good sense of guilty people. I know the evidence on paper makes you a prime candidate, but I just don't believe you did it and I don't think our chief seriously considers you, either. For one thing, it was done by someone very strong and most likely much taller than you, for another, your ex had some bad habits that put him in touch with some bad people." He frowned at her as he said, "It was an incredibly brutal death and I don't think you are capable of that kind of brutality."

A deep intake of breath, then Autumn said, "I don't want to think about that, but I'm glad you don't think I am guilty for whatever reason, so what's the problem with letting me tag along tomorrow?"

"Damn, you are relentless, you know that?"

"So, I've been told," she said.

"I know when I am beat. Pick you up at 9:00AM," he said with a sigh.

"Smart move," she said.

They went back inside, and a shadow moved in the back of the alley before it melted into the darkness.

***

Josh heard his phone chirp and he checked the text. It said, *"Did you tell your mom?"* --Timmy.

A glance at his mother. They were eating pizza at the big island in their kitchen. The kitchen was ginormous, just like the rest of the house, but they pretty much lived at this island or in their separate bedrooms on opposite ends of the house.

Josh's mom picked the house up in an auction and planned on making a lot of money when she sold it in a couple of years. She had lists of all the repos and knew the right people at the banks to schmooze.

His mom was so completely absorbed with her laptop that she didn't notice a large glob of cheese slide from her piece of pizza to her white pants. "Mom," he said, and when she looked up at him, he pointed to her pants.

"Damn." She put her slice down and headed for the laundry room.

His thumbs flew as he texted a reply, *"No moron! Keep your mouth shut."* –Josh

Almost immediately his phone chirped with Timmy's reply, *"We got to tell."* –Timmy

"*NO WAY!*" Josh followed the shouted text with a frowning red-faced emoji, then hit send and again it chirped almost instantly.

"*Pictures of bodies?????*" –Timmy

"*NOT REAL!*" His thumbs shook as he hit send. Timmy was going to break. He just knew it, and his mom was going to kill him. He sent another, "Photoshopped!" –Josh

Chirp. "*What if??????*" With a horrified face emoji with a big round mouth and eyes. -Timmy

"*Had it wrong. Place isn't empty. Dude's rich and owns house. It's on the downlow. A BIG DEAL. Not messin with. TOAST. We'll be toast!*" Followed with prayer hands emoji. -Josh

Chirp, "*Dude?*" –Timmy

"*Grounded for life...Maybe jail*!" Poop emoji. -Josh

Silence, then chirp, "*Ok*" With a sad face emoji after it.-Timmy

"*Stop texting. Talk later. CLEAR HISTORY!*" Josh turned his phone to silent and placed it face down on the island as he picked up another piece of pizza.

Those pictures were crazy bad, but who knew where they came from? The guy could be into some dark 50 shades type porn for all Josh knew.

What he did know was that he never, ever wanted his mom to know he and Timmy spent the entire summer breaking into the houses and ripping off the people she was responsible for. Not only would she kill and ground him, and it would ruin her career, Josh couldn't stand the thought of letting her down. His father hurt her so badly when he walked out of their lives, and for what? Some young piece of ass not that much older than Josh. He just couldn't let her get hurt again.

He gazed at his mother as she returned to her laptop and pizza. She smiled at him and happily started chowing down again. She may appear aggressive and strong, but since his dad left, she was fragile, and her real estate career was the only thing that made her smile, so he would not take that from her. *No way.*

Chapter 11

Autumn stood on her front porch with her eyes glued to the entrance of her driveway. When she spotted Dylan's SUV she moved to the first step, waved, hesitated a moment, and as he waved back, she headed down the rest of the steps and approached the car.

His ride was a light blue, older model Honda CRV. The metallic color reflected the morning light without a speck of dust or mud. It was not what she pictured him driving. She wasn't exactly sure what she expected, but it wasn't an impeccable 7-year-old SUV.

"How many miles do you have on it?" she said as she slid into the passenger side and slipped on her seatbelt.

"120,000 and change," he replied with a smile.

Did she hear pride in his voice? she thought, as she said, "That's mine," as she nodded toward the carport on the other side of her house at her 10-year-old pickup truck. "200,000 miles, but who's counting?" She shrugged and grinned.

"You are, and you win," he said, laughed, then added, "So, where's the pooch?"

"Fed, walked, and sleeping in her bed," she said, then added, "How far is it to Jan Miller's house?"

"About 20 miles." He backed the SUV around and headed up her driveway. "Shouldn't take too long, but we don't know how long it will take once we get there." He paused where the driveway met the road and asked, "Do you think the dog will be okay alone for most of the day?"

Autumn said, "Sure, she has really settled in. I thought it might be too confusing for her if we took her to her home and her mom wasn't there." She knew what he was really asking-- *Should they take Sadie along in case they found her owner and she wanted her dog back.* Autumn broke eye contact and looked toward the main road as she thought, *I will have a hard enough time giving Sadie up, so buying a little more time won't hurt anything.* She concentrated on the road ahead as Dylan left her driveway and headed out of the lake community toward the main highway.

The thick foliage stayed with them long after they left the small lake community and the forested area around the main highway provided a lush backdrop for their trip. The North Carolina scenery was full of color as they moved down the road; red, bright orange, yellow, and green was equally dispersed throughout the trees. She felt a thrill of anticipation. *Fall is here.*

Autumn was her favorite time of year, so maybe her adoptive mother chose her name wisely. She had no memory of her life before her parents adopted her, she didn't even remember the adoption, it seemed like she had always been with them. Her parents said that she was given to a church orphanage where they first met her. It almost sounded like a tale straight out of a gothic novel, but Autumn felt like it was kismet because her parents were wonderful, and she felt blessed to have come into their lives.

They told the story of her adoption to her many times during her life and she remembered everything they said. Now, with the Autumn foliage as a backdrop, she couldn't help but think about the way she got her name. She leaned her head against the window and her mother's words swirled in her mind, "*You were old enough to talk, but you refused to utter a word. You would frown and stare this intense gaze at whoever was talking to you. Your father said you had an 'old soul,' but I thought you must have had a hard time of it.*" Her mom always finished the story with, "*It was October when the adoption came through, so I called you my little Autumn prize. When you heard the word, Autumn, you smiled for the first time, so the name stayed. You see, you chose your own name."*

They traveled in silence with Autumn lost in thought until Dylan pulled off the highway and onto an exit that took them into a small farming community. She sat up and began looking around. Pickup trucks and SUV's dominated the downtown area as they passed through it. They stopped at the singular traffic light and Autumn noticed a hardware store with an adjacent parking lot filled with farm implements and tractors. Next to it was a farmer's market. She leaned forward and viewed baskets of fresh vegetables, fruits, and even hanging containers filled with fall flowers.

"Maybe we can stop there on the way back," Dylan said.

Autumn smiled. "That would be nice," she replied. The light changed, and they crawled through the rest of the town at the posted speed limit of 30mph. Autumn gazed at Dylan as he drove. He was wearing a blue denim work shirt and jeans with white tennis shoes. He was smooth shaven, but his hair was still just a little scruffy, and she wondered if he was dressed to fit into the community, or if this was who he really was. "I bet this is very different than your life in Chicago," she said.

"Yes, it is," he said. "I lived in the city not the burbs, and it wasn't far from the neighborhood I grew up in, but that's exactly why I took this job. I wanted a complete change."

"Why?" The word slipped out before she could filter it. A sideways glance from him and he gripped the steering wheel a little tighter.

"I have some wonderful memories of Chicago and a big family still living there, but I needed something different." A pause, then he said, "Honestly, coming here was a matter of survival."

"Listen, sorry about asking and you don't have to talk about whatever drove you here. I like to know what's behind the curtain on folks and sometimes I am a little too blunt," she said.

"It's okay. At least you asked me straight up instead of whispers when I walk into a room and then silence. You will eventually hear about it anyway, Lake Phillips is such a small community and like most little towns, everyone knows everything about everyone. A cliché, but it's true."

"I bet they have a lot to talk about with me. Especially after everything that's happened to me since I got here."

His lips twitched. "It's probably the first time they've given me a rest, so, thank you." He glanced at her then back at the windshield, before he said, "I'm the tragic new guy from the city who drinks too much." A sigh. "I'm also the cop who watched his partner get shot and die in front of him."

Autumn gasped and said, "Oh, man, I'm sorry. I thought it might be a tough divorce or something - I had no idea."

"Yeah, well, you *were* about the only one in town who didn't know, so you would've heard about it soon enough. My fault for bringing attention to it by drinking too much and being a royal ass most of the time. Talk about a cliché - I fit right in."

"You were a royal ass to me, so you played your part well, but I didn't make it any easier for you by being so prickly," Autumn said. He turned the SUV down a tree lined street with craftsman style houses and brick bungalows that looked like they were straight out of the 50's or 60's. "Is this her street?" she asked.

"Yes, we are almost there," he said, then continued with, "look for 201."

They both gazed at the houses looking for street numbers as he slowed the car even more, then he said, "There it is," when they saw the numbers posted on a mailbox. He pulled into the driveway which consisted of two strips of concrete with grass on either side and down the middle. Autumn chuckled; it looked like a little landing strip.

He eased up the driveway until they were parallel to the front porch. Dylan let the motor idle as they gazed at the red brick one story bungalow home. The house felt empty. Newspapers were stacked by the front door and a note was stuck in the corner of the storm door. "It doesn't look like she has been here for a while," Autumn said.

Dylan nodded and killed the engine. "Maybe she is on vacation," he said.

They got out of the car and approached the front door as neither of them spoke. As they got closer, Autumn could see the note was from a delivery service. It appeared they had tried to deliver a package several times but gave up until she called them. "It doesn't look promising," Autumn mumbled.

"Maybe she is on a trip and whoever was watching the dog and house let her down," Dylan said, but his eyes brimmed with disbelief. "I'll interview her neighbors to see if they have heard from her or know where she is."

"Okay, maybe I'll check around back."

"Remember, we are not here in an official capacity, so don't do anything illegal," he said as his eyes narrowed.

"I won't, I just want to see if her car is here, or if it looks like someone might have broken in."

"Okay, then I'll come with you," he said as he headed off the porch and turned toward the back of the house. "The neighbors can wait."

"You don't trust me?" Autumn asked.

"No."

She laughed and said, "Well, at least you are honest."

The back gate was standing open to a fully fenced, but slightly overgrown back yard. A rickety detached garage was at the very back of the property and a dust covered Toyota sedan sat in front of it. They glanced at each other and Dylan went through the gate and approached the back door. Autumn followed and had to quicken her steps to keep up with his long strides. She frowned and thought, *He doesn't seem to be moving stiffly now.*

The back door was divided into two sections, the bottom half was solid wood, and the upper half had a dozen small window panes, but the glass section was covered with a white linen curtain, so they couldn't see into the house.

Dylan rapped his knuckles on the wooden frame of the door and it edged inward. Not only was it unlocked, it was slightly ajar. He poked his head into the space and called, "Hello, Miss Miller?" A glance back at Autumn as he called even louder, "Police, just checking with you about your dog, Sadie." *Silence.* He moved into the house and repeated, "Hello? Police. Are you home, Miss Miller?" He held his hand up for Autumn to remain outside.

I thought this wasn't official, Autumn thought and frowned at his retreating form, and then followed him inside. He turned and scowled at her, but she smiled and kept coming. He shrugged and eased further into the house.

 They moved through a mudroom and into a small vintage kitchen with low ceilings. The bright black and white checkered tile floor, original cabinets painted white, and an enormous white farmhouse sink belied the thin coat of dust that was on the countertops and the pots with molding food that were in the sink.

The room was a vintage decorator dream kitchen that looked as if someone had fled from it in the middle of a meal. There was even a half-eaten bowl of dog food on the tile floor that had white fuzzy mold on it and several dead bugs on their backs around it. Autumn felt a chill move along her spine and wrinkled her nose at the smell trapped in the tight space.

They remained silent but kept going into the next room. It was a separate dining room and held another strange scene. The table was set for a romantic dinner for two. Half-filled wine glasses, plates with uneaten, molding food, and candles that had burned down to the tops of the candlesticks with gobs of wax flowing onto the white linen tablecloth.

One of the wineglasses was almost empty and had lipstick staining the side. The lipstick glass was at a table setting that had its chair turned on its side. Autumn was barely breathing, and the room was so quiet she felt as if she could hear her heart as it beat in her chest. It felt like they had walked onto the set of a play, but the actors were missing.

Dylan examined the table, then looked toward the corner dining room hutch. He walked over and bent to examine a cluster of framed photos. As he stood back up and looked at Autumn he was pale. "What?" she whispered, then walked over and looked at the pictures.

It was a series of family photos. They were typical for any home; nothing was ominous. But as Autumn gazed at them she felt the blood drain from her face and her head felt light. A young woman with her dog in most of them, and some more with an older couple who were probably her parents. The pictures had to be Jan Miller and Sadie, but it could have just as easily been Autumn and Sadie. At first glance, she was the one in the photos. She looked back up at Dylan and froze, then whispered, "What does this mean?"

He shook his head and said, "I'm not sure." He gazed toward the living room, then back to Autumn and handed her the car keys as he said, "I want you to go to the car and wait for me."

"But,"

"Now," he said as he interrupted her, then he slipped a gun from a holster hidden under his jeans at his ankle. He looked toward the living room and took a step, and then added, "Please."

Autumn sighed, glanced at the table, back to the pictures, then nodded at his back and left the room.

She moved through the kitchen and mud room, and when she reached the back yard, she stopped and took several deep breaths. She hesitated only a moment, then headed straight for the car.

The air chilled her back as she walked, and she realized she had sweated through her T-shirt in several places. At the SUV, she jumped in and engaged the locks before she turned to look back at the house. She couldn't see anything through the curtained windows, but she imagined Dylan moving through the rooms still looking for the elusive Jan Miller. With the amount of blood on Sadie, Autumn's imagination ratcheted from one awful scene to another as she anticipated what he might find.

It was the pictures that got to her more than the creepy tableau in the kitchen or dining room. She could easily be Jan Miller's sister; they had the same auburn hair, similar build and facial features.

She rotated her head as she tried to look for anyone approaching the SUV, then shivered as she thought about the pictures again. *Hell, admit it, Brennan, at first glance you wondered how a picture of you with Sadie got in Jan Miller's house.* She stared out of the front windshield and whispered, "What the hell is going on?"

After a few minutes Dylan emerged from the gate. He had his cell phone to his ear and he was speaking in a low voice to someone. He shook his head at her and she realized he had not found Sadie's owner. *They probably never will, she thought.*

Chapter 12

Autumn slid down to her knees and gripped Sadie on both sides of her face. "I'm sorry, girl, but I don't think your momma is coming back," she whispered as she felt a tear run down her cheek, then she rubbed the dog's head and hugged her. Autumn stood, and then added, "Don't worry; you will always have a home with me and I promise to take good care of you and not let anyone else hurt you." The dog responded with what sounded like, "Mumph," as she gazed up at her.

Autumn felt watched, so she turned and noticed Ying and Yang silently staring at them from the entrance to the kitchen. Richard told her that the unblinking *cat stare* creeped him out, but to Autumn, it spoke volumes. She sometimes pictured the cats as more intelligent beings trying to send messages telepathically, other times, she thought they might have no thought process going on at all. She laughed aloud. *Feed me human,* was probably their message right now. "All, right, I know it's dinner time," she said.

As she walked toward the kitchen she decided that whatever they were thinking, especially when it was directed toward Richard, probably involved cursing and sarcasm. Autumn smiled when she realized she was thinking of Richard as he was in life instead of only his violent death.

In the kitchen, she filled the cat bowls and placed their food in front of them before setting a full bowl of food in front of Sadie. The cats began their slow, deliberate chewing, while Sadie attacked the food as if it were an enemy, complete with a low growl. Autumn smiled at them, then turned to look out of the kitchen window, but today, it was hard to find her usual comfort there.

It was dusk, and the lake looked like a smooth, dark mirror as the last of the sun's rays angled over its surface. A family of geese ambled down the slope of her yard toward the water's edge, and she could hear them honking as they gorged on hidden morsels in the tall grass as they went. Autumn sighed and reached for a beer from the cooler, then drew back to the window as she sipped the brew.

The day was both satisfying and excruciating. Dylan was surprisingly easy to be with, even with the agonizing discoveries at Jan Miller's home. They skipped the farmers market; neither of them was in the mood after the eerie scenes at the house, and, after all the police presence and questioning, it was late by the time they left her neighborhood.

What had happened in that house? How could a romantic dinner have gone so wrong? There was no blood on the scene. At least there was that. So, how did Sadie get so much blood on her and how had she gotten the twenty plus miles to Autumn's dock? She felt her head begin to ache, so she took another sip of her beer and closed her eyes as she felt it slide down her throat. It was foolish to keep going over and over the same thoughts. She was creating more questions than answers each time she tried to figure it out. Again, she felt like she was missing something that was obvious.

She opened her eyes again. A glance at Sadie. The dog had finished her meal and was lapping an after-dinner drink out of their pet fountain. When Autumn spotted the animal water fountain on her favorite internet shopping site, she had to order it. Fresh water pumped through a filter and out of a little plastic yellow flower. It was adorable and practical at the same time. Even picky Ying and Yang loved drinking from the contraption. The normalcy of the scene comforted her.

Her eyes drew back to the window. *What happened to Jan Miller?* The thought kept running through Autumn's mind like a spinning wheel. She shook her head as if she could physically dislodge the stream of thought. Instead, her mind went back to wondering where

Sadie's previous owner was and if the blood on the dog was hers, was she dead? She grimaced. *I can't believe I'm thinking of Jan Miller as dead.*

The memory of Sadie sitting on Autumn's dock and staring at the water sent another cold chill down Autumn's spine. The dog had acted as if she was drugged and there was moldy dog food with dead bugs around it at the house. *Did someone drug Sadie? And if they did, did they drug Jan Miller as well?* She turned away from the window and the thought she was avoiding the most popped into her head, *What is the deal with the resemblance between me and Jan Miller?*

It had taken hours for the police to process the missing woman's house, then Autumn had to make a statement to the sheriff's department as they kept asking her questions. *Why was she at Jan Miller's house? Had she ever met her? Did she know why the dog was on her property so far away from its home?* Dylan had helped her on several of the questions, then insisted on taking her home. She was grateful he intervened because she was about to lose her temper with them, and that would not have ended up well.

Not only the questions about Jan Miller swirled in her head, she was also trying not to think about why Richard had such a violent death. She expected an overdose, or car accident, but this? And how, if at all, was his death connected to the missing Jan Miller? She shook her head again to clear her thoughts. "Just stop!" She said as she leaned on the counter and shut her eyes. "Maybe a soak in the tub will help," she mumbled.

Autumn opened her eyes and turned to leave the kitchen, but as she passed through the dining room, something caught her attention from the corner of her eye. She stopped and gazed at the picture window. *What?* There was nothing unusual with what she saw. Same lake, same geese, same houses across the lake. But something had flashed light. She moved closer and her eyes swept the lake surface, then the area across the lake.

Where was it coming from? She examined the houses on the other side of the lake. She saw a flash of a spark of light from the big white house opposite her window. The house's curtains were closed, but it had looked like a metallic glint that came from the basement where the curtains met. As hard as she stared, she couldn't see anything concrete, and the flash did not reappear.

A shrug, the house was far away, and it looked like it came from the lower level under a porch, so it was not likely she had seen anything, but she still drew her new curtains closed and stopped to check the alarm before she went up to draw herself a bath. She was getting entirely too spooked over nothing, but after all that had happened, it wasn't surprising.

The hot water was just what she needed. After Autumn slipped into the warm bath, she stretched and then pulled a wet wash cloth over her eyes as she rested her head against the back of the porcelain tub. The tub was big and old and took her back in time to when she was a girl taking a bubble bath.

A noise. She sat up with a splash and listened for the creak of a floorboard. But whatever she had heard didn't repeat, so she leaned back and relaxed again. It was a difficult day and she needed to stop thinking about it before she was jumping at shadows. Autumn leaned back again against the smooth porcelain and took some deep breaths as she thought about how beautiful this old house was going to be when she finished remodeling it and the long day began to slip away.

***

Michelle, or Autumn, as everyone else called her, was at her kitchen window once again. *She drinks too much beer*, Rowen thought as he watched her through the telescope lens. He wanted to introduce her to wine, and not just regular wine, but fine wine. He was sure she would like it much better than that cheap swill she was consuming.

There were many things he wanted to share with her. Not only the finer things in life, but her real and true name, Michelle. He hated hearing her called by that made up name and couldn't wait to tell her who she really was. *I should make a list of everything I need to share,* he thought.

Rowen loved his lists and the way they comforted him. Just going back over all the items and crossing off the ones he had already accomplished made his pulse slow down and head quit buzzing. Sometimes he felt as if his head would explode with the noise of his thoughts as they moved in lightning speed through his brain. Writing his thoughts and ideas down organized and quieted them.

She disappeared from the kitchen window, so he moved the telescope and sighed when he picked her up in the dining room. She was so beautiful. He watched her heading toward the stairs to the second story, but then she stopped and turned toward him.

As she approached the big picture window he sucked in his breath. She stared straight at him. It was as if she could see him across the lake without assistance, but he knew better, so he held his ground and kept watching her. It was both excruciating and exhilarating.

A moment of intent staring, then she closed the curtains and the connection was gone. It felt almost electric and left Rowen tingling all over. *I wonder if she sensed me?*

When she was looking right at him he could hardly breathe. The game kept getting better and better now that he had Michelle back in his life. He could not wait to be facing her without a telescope or drone's lenses between them. *What will it feel like?* he thought. *After all this time, will she remember me?* He tilted his head and smiled. He could wait until the time was right. After all, there was something to be said for secret viewing. Being invisible was such a delicious pleasure. But still, he couldn't wait to see how proud she was of him and all his accomplishments. He was so much stronger now. He wondered if she would notice it right away.

A glance at his watch and Rowen turned away from the telescope and went into his bedroom to dress for his date. As he moved through his closet he touched and studied each suit until he chose the perfect one. The suits were all tailor made of the finest materials available and carefully hung and sealed in zippered bags. He had to unzip the bags slightly to feel the fabric, but he enjoyed making his choice both visually and by touch.

His outfit choice was all part of the ritual. As were the items he kept in a trunk in the back of the spacious closet. He glanced at the trunk but decided to leave his choice from it until after he met his date.

He carried his suit into the bedroom and thought about watching Michelle, but as he started to change he paused for a moment and turned his head to look toward the bedroom door. He shook his head. No time to watch his videos. He needed to get ready and his schedule must be kept. Rowen began dressing again.

As he sat to pull on his shoes, he reached down to touch the soft Italian leather. His finger left a tiny mark, so he frowned and grabbed a cloth. As he buffed it out as his thoughts turned back to watching Michelle. He liked the pictures and movies the drone created because they were fun to edit and review when she was out of his sight, but he had to admit he really liked going old school with the telescope. It made it seem like he was right in front of her.

The old movie, *Rear Window*, was his first inspiration. He saw it one night on the classics channel when he was just a kid and he felt an immediate connection to Hitchcock. *What a man—He was a genius with his films.* He watched every one of his movies after that and they were what helped him create his games. The movies made him feel as if he was spying through the camera lens, intentional on Hitchcock's part, and inspirational to Rowen. Daydreams that turned into reality were beyond ecstasy.

Watching Michelle with the telescope made him feel just like when he first saw Rear Window. It was as if he was in the room with her, only he was invisible. The drone movies were satisfying, but not electrifying like the telescope. Plus, when she got close to the drone he had to maneuver it home to avoid discovery, and with the telescope, he could keep watching her as long as she was exposed.

He shook his head and tried to get back on task. It was almost time for his date and he didn't want her to get impatient. He put Michelle out of his mind and thought about this stage of the game with his date. A calmness washed over him as he pictured how the evening would go. After all, anticipation and planning were the best parts of his games. Well, maybe not the best part, but it was still something he enjoyed and loved to savor.

Rowen did love to savor: good food, expensive wine, all the finer things, and most of all, the satisfaction of his game. The games he played brought him his own unique brand of gratification and it was amazing. He only wished he had discovered it when he was much younger. He shrugged. He did not have the finances to carry it to this level of perfection when he was younger, so it was just as well. He was now rich enough to do anything he wanted thanks to his startup company going public. For years he yearned for someone to share his secret game with---and now here she was. Everything was falling into place at last.

He put the finishing touches on his outfit and carefully examined himself in the full-length mirror; he was perfect. *What a lucky lady,* he thought. He went to his computer and opened the dating sight app and brought up the profile of the lovely lady he scheduled a date with. *Erin Watson.* He reached out and touched her face on the screen. This one was much better than the last one. She fit all his criteria. He exited the program and shut off his computer.

He made a quick trip to the big old steamer trunk he kept in the back of his closet. It seems he couldn't wait after all. He opened it and gazed at the multiple outfits sealed in plastic wrap. A bright shinny blue caught his attention. He pulled it out along with the matching shoe box and closed the trunk. Rowen eased open the closure and released the shimmery blue mini dress from its plastic wrap as he shook it and held it up for inspection. The blue polyester material covered in shimmering blue sequins didn't even need steaming. Ah, the power of polyester, he thought with a smirk as he draped the dress over his arm and held the shoes in his other hand. He left the plastic wrap on the closed trunk lid and headed out of the room.

He went down the long hallway and entered a small room where he carefully laid the dress on a cot and placed the matching platform heels beside it. "All set," he said, then he grinned, left the room, grabbed his go bag, and headed out the door.

Chapter 13

"Are you sure nobody is staying here?"

"Yes, for the hundredth time," Josh said without even trying to hide the exasperation in his voice.

"That's what you said at the last place and you know what happened there," Timmy said, as he followed Josh through the front door of the rambling two story house. "I'm still freaked out about those pictures. I know you said it was just some kind of internet porn and they were fake, but I've never seen that kind of stuff on any porn sites."

"I know, but just because you don't go to the dark web sites doesn't mean they don't exist. I'm telling you---my cousin says he has seen all kinds of weird bondage shit and what looks like much worse, but he said it's all fake, and he should know, he's a real big deal in computer programing."

"I don't know about that," Timmy said as he shook his head back and forth.

"It's true. He even showed me a couple of pics with naked women and handcuffs and whips and shit." Josh stopped in the foyer and said, "It wasn't my fault someone was living there because it was listed as empty on her spreadsheet. How was I to know she sold it? Besides, I made sure this house is unoccupied. I got her talking about it and she griped about how she hadn't been able to unload it on anyone. No one can afford it, so no more surprises."

"I guess," Timmy said with a frown.

"And this is the last one, I swear. We just need a little more money and we are set, otherwise, this has all been for nothing." Josh said, then flicked on his flashlight and Timmy did the same.

They stood in an enormous two-story entryway with a double staircase winding up from both sides of the front hall. The flooring of the foyer consisted of big shiny white square tiles and there was a gilded table in the middle of the hall with a golden statue of a winged angel in the middle of it. The boys looked at each other and laughed at the statue, then laughed even harder when their voices echoed in the cavernous entry hall. When they stopped laughing, they both aimed their lights beyond the hall into the next room and all the furniture was covered in white sheets. "See, empty," Josh said.

"It looks a little creepy to me," Timmy said, then asked, "Upstairs or down?"

"Let's start upstairs in the bedrooms. We'll have better luck if they have kids and they left some of their electronic toys. Rich bastards probably have sets of stuff everywhere they go; maybe we can even find a new X-box and then we can use our money just for gaming," Josh said, then headed toward the staircase on the left. He stood a little straighter and his voice lowered as he added, "Bet they won't even miss the crap we take."

Timmy laughed and started up the staircase on the right as he said, "Beat ya!"

Josh shook his head and said nothing but kept his same pace. He knew that Timmy's size and girth might help them with the school bullies, but there was no way he would beat Josh going up the stairs, even though he thought he was racing him. When Josh got to the second story landing, Timmy was only a few seconds behind him, but his face was flushed red, and Josh could hear him panting. "Next time, buddy," was all Josh said, then turned and started down the hallway.

The first bedroom they entered had nothing of interest, nor the next three, but at the end of the hall, they found a staircase leading to another floor. They followed it up and entered an enormous playroom. "Jackpot," Josh said, and Timmy whistled as they entered the room and gazed around.

I thought my house was ginormous; this one room is the same size as the entire first floor of my house, Josh thought. He took another step into the space and used his flashlight to sweep it from top to bottom. "Damn," he muttered. Although the center of the room had high ceilings, they slanted down steeply until the side walls didn't have much clearance; it was an oversized attic space dedicated to fun. His flashlight played along the sides of the room where tiny windows were covered with blackout curtains; it would be as dark as night in here during the day. A perfect place to forget what time it was.

But the best part, the part that made both boys grin and fist bump each other, was that it was full of sheet shrouded 'toys'. The silhouettes of several pinball machines, a ping pong table, and a foosball table stood out, but there were many more covered treasures Josh couldn't make out, so he started pulling the sheets off and yelled at each new discovery.

When they were half way across the room, both boys stopped and stared toward the very end of the room as their flashlights landed on their biggest prize, then they turned and nodded at each other before running toward it. Mounted on the end wall, was the biggest flat screen TV Josh had ever seen and it had game controls on the console below it. In front of it two rows of black leather recliners complete with cupholders resided. This was the holy grail they were searching for all summer long. A gamer's dream setup.

"I bet this stuff isn't covered with sheets because the dipshit caretaker my mom uses is a gamer. I met him a couple of times and he a total idiot tool, but he's cheap, so she keeps using him."

"Lucky dog," Timmy mumbled as he headed straight for the game console. "He gets paid to be a slacker."

"Yep, but guess what? So, do we," Josh said and laughed as he flopped down into one of the leather chairs, leaned back, and slid his leg over the cushy arm. "Plus, he left everything ready for us to use." He realized his laugh sounded high pitched like a girl's, but he didn't even care. He accepted the control Timmy handed him and laughed again. He found his bliss and he was with his best buddy to enjoy it. Life was sweet.

***

The water sloshed over the side of the tub as Autumn bolted upright into a sitting position. The room was dark and quiet, and it felt as if she was sitting in a tub full of ice.

The trill from her phone broke the silence and she realized that was what woke her. Autumn stood, but her feet slipped, so she grabbed the side of the tub, and then stepped out and wrapped a towel around her wet body as the persistent ringing continued. *How long was I asleep?* She thought as she reached blindly for the phone and then flipped on the bathroom light and grabbed it. "Hello?" she said.

"Hi, it's Dylan."

She realized she was shivering, so she switched the phone mode to speaker and placed it on the vanity. She slipped into her robe and sat on the side of the tub. "Oh, hi, uh, what time is it?" she said.

"Just before 7:00. Are you okay? You sound strange."

"I'm fine, uh, you're on speaker and there is an echo in here. I must have fallen asleep in the bath," her cheeks reddened as she realized what she had just said. Autumn shrugged, pushed her hair out of her eyes, and frowned at her toes; the nails were still painted a dark blue from sandal weather, but the color was faded and chipped in places. She blinked and gazed back at the phone and said, "Sorry, I must have had some really strange dreams because I'm having a hard time waking up." Autumn tried to remember what she was dreaming about, but it was a dark jumble. *Something weird about a chain locked around her ankle? Where did that come from?* she thought. She shook her head to clear it and pushed the dream away before she again said, "Sorry."

"Oh, no---I'm sorry I woke you, but after all that happened today, I, uh, I wanted to check on you. I'm not surprised you are having strange dreams with what has been going on." Dylan said.

"Thanks, that's really sweet of you, but I'm fine, and I needed to wake up," she said, but she held back the information that she was sleeping so long that the warm bath had turned into ice water and she was lucky she hadn't drowned. She rolled her eyes and pulled her robe tighter.

"Have you had dinner?" he asked.

"Uh, no," Autumn said as she ran her hand over her belly and felt a rumble. With their discovery at Jan Miller's house she forgot to eat lunch as well, so she realized she had not eaten since breakfast. *Forgotten to eat? Crazy!* Autumn thought. She was not someone who forgot meals and usually ate every three or four hours, so she was surprised she was even able to function at this point. "Actually, I am famished," she said.

"I was just going out for something to eat, would you like to join me?" Dylan asked.

Autumn stood and frowned at her reflection as she said, "That would be great because I am starving, but can you give me thirty minutes?" She leaned forward and shook her head at her reflection as she realized she was asking the impossible to make herself presentable in that amount of time, but tummy rumbles won, so she would do it.

"Sure, okay, I'll pick you up then."

Autumn disconnected, frowned at the mirror again, and then said, "Move it, sunshine," as she hurried into the bedroom to get dressed.

The Italian restaurant, appropriately named Vinny's, was warm and cozy and smelled like garlic bread and homemade pasta sauce. Autumn inhaled the heady scents and thought she might faint from hunger as she felt her mouth water. A sign at the front said, 'seat yourself,' so she swallowed hard and followed Dylan through the long narrow room until he reached the back and said, "Is this okay?" She nodded, and they slid into a booth with a red checkered table cloth and bread sticks in a jar. It was like something out of a 50's movie set in New York city, complete with low lighting with little lamps on all the tables and a Sinatra song playing in the background.

Autumn pulled off her sweater and felt her shoulders and neck relax for the first time in days. This was even better than the warm bath she had slipped into earlier. Maybe things were looking up at last.

The waiter came over to take their drink order almost as soon as they sat down. He was a robust middle-aged man with black curly hair and several neck rings of fat. He rested his hands on his round belly with a pen in one hand and a note pad in the other as he spoke to Dylan on a first name basis. Autumn became fascinated by the way the fat rings of his neck jiggled with each word. Dylan introduced them, and the man wiped his hands on his once white apron that now had little splatters of red sauce in several spots before he stuck his hand out to her and said, "Good to meet you, Miss Autumn," in a thick New York accent.

"And you, Vinny," Autumn said. After they both ordered Sangria and Vinny moved off to the next guest, she picked up the menu and grinned.

"What?" Dylan asked.

"Nothing," she said, then lowered the menu and added, "It's this place--it's great."

Dylan laughed. "I felt the same way the first time I came here and still do after dozens of visits. Vinny is from the Bronx and this is his place; no kidding. It sounds like something a PR person would have created, but Vinny is the real deal. He works hard to make everyone feel as if they were sitting in his kitchen and a part of his family."

Autumn laughed and said, "Okay, after meeting him that totally fits."

Another waiter came over to bring them their drinks and take their food order, and then they sipped Sangria and exchanged their thoughts about Lake Phillips, Autumn's life in Nashville, and Dylan's life in Chicago, nothing deep, just bits of 'getting to know you' weaving through the conversation.

Autumn leaned back on the cushy red booth and chatted as the wine loosened her tongue. She usually hated this part, which was one of the reasons she avoided dating, not that this was a date, but the awkward beginnings of getting to know a man, at least for her, was usually filled with red flag surprises, but this felt different. She gazed at her dinner companion and sucked in a breath as it dawned on her that it wasn't the circumstance that was different, it was Dylan.

He was not like any of the men she attempted to connect with in her limited, awkward testing of the single world. She smiled and tilted her head as she also realized she wanted to know more about him. *Now that is different,* she thought. Even with their previously awkward professional meetings, for the first time since she left Richard, she wasn't hearing anything that made her want to run.

As the conversation paused, Autumn said, "The last few days have been pretty surreal and awful. Being here tonight is a nice change, so thank you. For the first time in days I'm finding myself not bracing for what disaster is coming next."

"I know what you mean. I felt as if the walls were closing in on me when I left Chicago. It was like if I didn't leave, my world was going to end."

"Your partner's death?" she asked.

"Yes, mostly---but, it was more than that. I come from a long line of cops and a big family who understood what it means to lose a partner in the line of duty, but what made it so much worse was that Kate, my partner, was also my partner when we weren't at work."

"Oh," Autumn said, but she wasn't surprised at the revelation. Something about his tone when he spoke of her gave the impression that she was a very important part of his life.

"We kept it quiet, so we could still work together, but I think everyone might have guessed. I wasn't sure, but I couldn't stand the look in their eyes every time they saw me; the pity just got to be too much. I felt like a widower, but I also felt I had no rights to claim that role. It was as if the lie we were living somehow betrayed our feelings; betrayed her importance in my life. I know her death colored the way I saw everything, but suddenly, the city I once loved, the people who surrounded me, all of it took on the proportions of a giant monster: too big, too noisy, and too much."

"I get that…" Autumn said. She felt her hand moving toward him, but the spell was broken as the waiter brought their food and she pulled it back. They remained quiet and subdued as he placed the huge steaming bowls of pasta and sauce in front of them. She nodded when he offered her parmesan cheese, and then let him bury the red sauce in a mound of white cheese before she nodded again for him to stop. Once the waiter left she said, "This looks amazing."

"I've never had better," Dylan said. He smiled, and he looked like a different person. His eyes sparkled and the creases around his mouth seemed smoother. Autumn thought that it must be difficult for him not to have anyone to share his heavy secret with. No wonder he was earning a reputation of a brooding man with a past.

Autumn felt a chill as she realized that she was in much the same situation after her divorce. Her best friend had moved away, and then her marriage became filled with only 'his friends and band mates.' When their marriage fell apart, she not only lost him, but their band mates, *and* friends. She was instantly isolated with no one she could share her feelings with. She silently vowed not to have that happen again.

After they ate in silence for a while lost in their own thoughts, Autumn paused and said, "I don't know what I'm supposed to feel about Richard's death. I no longer loved him, but I once did very much, and the thought of what happened to him horrifies and haunts me. I can't seem to stop visualizing what his death must have been like or what he felt at the end." She shivered and pulled her sweater up over her shoulders.

Dylan nodded and said, "I'm sorry Officer Wilson painted that picture for you. Believe me, I understand how you feel all too well. Violence like that is hard to process and it takes time for our minds to wrap around it." He paled slightly, and Autumn assumed he was thinking of his partner, then he said, "It is hard, but it gets better, or at least it changes, but I don't want to ever get accustomed to it." He took a sip of his drink then cleared his throat and said, "I understand that Richard's brother claimed the body and will be taking him back to Nashville for burial."

"Yes, I spoke with him." She paused in eating, set down her fork and gazed at Dylan as she said, "I haven't decided if I will go back for the funeral."

"Whatever you decide will be the right thing," he said and then his phone chirped, and he glanced at the readout. "It's work, do you mind if I take it?"

"No, not at all," she said as she picked up her fork again.

He listened and nodded a few times, then said, "Alright, I'll be there soon." He frowned, signaled to the waiter and then turned to her and said, "I'm sorry, but we will have to get these to go. We might have caught a break with a string of burglary cases I've been working on. They just got a call from the caretaker of a vacant house that had a silent alarm go off and that's these guys MO."

"Hey, no problem," she replied as she gathered her things and the waiter took their dishes away to pack their food for them. She pulled out a twenty and laid it on the table, but Dylan shook his head.

110

"I've got this," he said.

"No, I'll pay my part. You've done enough with taking me to check out Jan Miller's house," she said, then added, "I should be picking up your tab as well."

He smiled and said, "I know I said I wanted to check on you when I called tonight, and that much was true, but the trip to her house, and dinner was on my own time and because, well, the truth is I enjoy your company." He let out a breath and continued with, "I will graciously accept your part for dinner if you do not want to consider this a, well, uh, a date, but if you would consider it, I asked, so I'll pay."

Autumn was quiet a moment, then nodded and picked up the twenty and tucked it back into her wallet. "Thank you," she nodded and said, and then added, "Next time it will be my treat and I will ask. I really want to talk more about what we found today at Jan Miller's house. I know neither of us mentioned it, but I have to say that it wasn't the state of her place that got into my head, but my resemblance to Jan Miller. At first glance those photos could be me and, I must admit, it is creeping me out a little. I want to explore what it means, if anything."

"*Right?* Yes, that set me back, too." Dylan said, then stood and moved down the aisle as Autumn followed him. About half way to the door he paused and turned toward her and said, "I want to talk it out also, but you had me at 'next time,' especially after me cutting out so quickly tonight."

Autumn laughed, and they headed for the front where Vinney was waiting with two white containers. Each were marked with their names written across the top. *Why does it feel like we have done this a dozen times?* Autumn thought as she found herself grinning.

As they left the restaurant and headed for Dylan's car, Autumn found the cozy comfort she felt in the restaurant seemed to stay with her. Although she didn't initially think of their dinner as a 'date' until Dylan mentioned it, she was pleased it turned into one.

If she was being honest with herself, which was something she always tried to do, she felt her annoyance with him turn into a strange flirtation sometime before they arrived at Jan Miller's house, maybe even when they were still at Cowboys. Her previous disastrous attempts at dating after her divorce was great material for her songs, but this was different. *This feels right.*

Autumn wasn't sure it would go anywhere, but as he opened her car door and she slid into the passenger side, it felt natural and organic, just like their conversation. She considered herself an independent woman who embraced her solitude, but she found herself wanting him to open doors for her, and that was unusual, hell, that was unheard of. She didn't even have to bite her tongue to keep from saying, "I can open it myself." The words simply weren't waiting to tumble out like they usually were.

Autumn gazed at him as he got into the driver's side and started the car and thought, *Yes, I do want to find out more about Dylan McAlister.* She leaned her head back and relaxed as he drove her home.

Chapter 14

Erin Watson scrutinized the woman staring at her from the bathroom mirror. "What are you doing, Erin?" she asked herself. She was doing that a lot lately. She was a happy person, not a ball of sunshine all the time, but genuinely happy with her life. So why did she agree to meet some stranger she met on the internet? And why in the world did she agree to let him come to her house to pick her up for their, *oh god,* date?

She ran her fingers through her wavy red hair and shrugged, then turned away from her image and headed downstairs. As she descended the wooden steps she gripped the railing and took in each detail of the two-story foyer of her townhouse as if seeing it for the first time. *This will be his view if I decide to allow him past the front door,* she thought. A pause on the last step accompanied by a deep sigh. "Why, Erin, why?" she mumbled.

The entryway to the townhouse was impeccable and impressive. She knew she had to have the home the minute she saw it, and within a month, despite a bidding war, it was hers.

The house had all the right updates, but they didn't strip its century old character away. It was exactly what she wanted, and she loved coming home to it every night. Even after five years it still thrilled her to know it was hers.

Erin worked hard to get to where she was in her life. Her mother told her, much too often, that she sacrificed her personal life to achieve this lofty living space, a corner office at her law firm, and a healthy bank account. Her mother thought she was criticizing her, but Erin took it as a compliment and was filled with pride each time she said it. *It's not a sacrifice if I enjoy every minute of it, mom.*

Erin loved her work. She loved her morning run, then scurrying to shower and hitting the office before anyone else arrived. She loved forgetting the time and consistently being the last person to leave at night. She did make one sacrifice, though, and that was sharing her life with a fur baby. Erin loved animals; dogs, cats, rabbits, *whatever*, but didn't think it was fair to any creature in need of companionship to have so little of her time. She knew she could get dog walkers or use a day care service, but *really?* Wouldn't that be a little selfish with her hours?

She compromised by getting a giant fish tank in her study. A cute young man came once a week to keep it sparkling and the fish didn't care if she worked 70 or 80 hours a week. They just wanted their sprinkle of fish food every morning and they seemed happy to swim away the rest of their day with their little fish meetings under the fake rock bridge and travelling through the cute plastic tunnel and sea plants.

Erin loved her life, her freedom, her work, her colorful fish; so how in the hell did she wind up on a dating site? *My friend, Jennifer, that's how.* The crazy bitch created a dating profile for Erin and posted it without her knowledge. Erin freaked out when she saw it and it nearly ended their friendship, but then she read all the responses in the 'in' box and curiosity drove her to look further. Well, curiosity and her insatiable urge to succeed even if it was garnering the most eligible catch on a dating site.

So here she was; dressed in her best networking outfit. Not too sexy, not too boardroom, just right for a first date. *Oh, god,* she thought as she moved over to the mirror above the hall table that was a catchall for her keys, purse, and mail as she entered the townhouse each evening. One more quick check and she was satisfied. Her clear, smooth skin, thanks to all those hours inside with little sun, made her appear much younger than she was, but she still never lied about her age, so thank goodness Jennifer had honored that on the fake profile.

The man who was coming to pick her up looked great on paper. Relatively handsome, tall, successful, smart and quite rich, which she garnered from the background check she did on him, and he was self-made, or so it appeared from his profile.

She met him for a quick coffee first, simply to see if she could tolerate a full-blown date before she agreed to it. Normally she would have met him at the restaurant for dinner instead of allowing him to pick her up, but since she fully vetted him, and nothing popped up, she agreed they would go together. So here she was, just like a nervous schoolgirl, waiting for him to come to her front door.

Erin told everyone she didn't need a man, marriage, or children in her life. She had her girlfriends, her family, and the life she always dreamed of, but still, she liked to stay open to possibilities. Romantic love never entered her life; sex, lust, fun, yes, but not romance. She wasn't sure *love* was in the realm of things for her and she was okay with that. Although the hype was 'you can have it all,' Erin didn't believe it, and she was happy to settle for rich and loving her work, but still—*possibilities*—

The doorbell rang. She turned to look at the door, took a quick intake of breath, and moved toward it. At the door she paused with her hand on the doorknob, pushed back her shoulders, straightened her spine, then smiled and pulled the door open.

"Good evening, Erin, nice to see you again," he said. He extended a thick bouquet of flowers and added, "I saw these and thought of you."

She accepted the flowers, nodded and replied, "Oh, you didn't need to do that, but thank you." She glanced at his other hand and frowned. He held a small black gym bag.

He followed her gaze and said, "Oh, sorry. I came from meeting with a client and had to stop at the gym to shower and change. May I leave this here while we go to dinner? I don't want to forget it in the Uber or drag it around at dinner."

Her shoulders relaxed. He was a kindred spirit; working right up until time for them to meet. She said, "Sure, why don't you come inside, and I'll put these in water before we go." She took a step back and held the door open as Rowen entered the townhouse.

Chapter 15

As Dylan pulled into the driveway he could see the security guy slumped on the driver's side of the van with his lights and engine off. He was barely visible in the cloudy moonless night and an occasional glow as he took a drag from a cigarette was the only indication he was still alive.

Dylan sat with his car idling for a moment as he watched him, then he pulled farther into the long circular driveway and parked directly behind the van. His car smelled of Italian food. He glanced at the takeout container on the front seat and it reminded him of his ruined date. He frowned and killed his engine, and then got out as he stood watching the driver for a moment longer, but the man barely moved.

The driver's head was cocked to one side as a trail of smoke wafted out of the van's open window. At least it was tobacco Dylan sniffed as it floated across the space instead of pot.

His cop radar was buzzing as he observed the sloppy so-called security detail. If he didn't already suspect the burglaries were teens, this guy might make it to the top of his list of suspects, still, he would keep him in mind.

As Dylan watched the glowing tip of the man's cigarette and his complete disregard for what was going on around him, the possibilities of his involvement multiplied. The caretaker was privy to information about houses at the lake and Dylan's first impression screamed that he either knew what was happening and didn't care, or at the very least he was ineffective. Even if he wasn't the one pulling off the thefts, he might be leaking information about the houses for profit, or out of stupidity.

There should be some sort of reaction from the security guard on Dylan's arrival. He expected a greeting to acknowledge his presence and maybe an offer to escort him through the house, but the idiot continued to sit in the van smoking his cigarette. *How can he not know I am here?* Dylan thought as he shook his head in disbelief.

If Dylan was a burglar, he could have come and gone without a challenge. Hell, he could have put a bullet in the jackass's brain for that matter. Is he really that incompetent, or does he know he has nothing to fear because he is, or is connected to, the actual thief?

Dylan made his fist form a gun and silently pulled the trigger as he thought, *It's a good thing I'm not the bad guy.* He shrugged and eased up to the open driver's side window, and then flicked the beam of his flashlight into the van as he asked in his deepest voice, "Have you been inside, yet?"

The driver jumped and twirled toward Dylan as he simultaneously pulled out his ear buds and said, "Shit, man, don't sneak up on someone like that."

That answers the question of why he didn't hear Dylan's car as he approached the van. Dylan thought about making a snide remark that he thought the lights and engine of his car would have given him away, but instead he repeated his question, "Have you been inside?"

"No, man, I was waiting for you guys," the security guard said as he leaned forward and snubbed out his cigarette into an ashtray overflowing with ash and butts.

As he was bent forward Dylan eyed the *Lake Phillips House Care and Security* logo embroidered on the back of his blue jump suit. He chuckled as he thought, *He looks more like a parolee than security personnel.* Slicked back greasy hair, reeking of nicotine, and eyes that darted around a little too much made Dylan wonder how he got this job. Maybe he was somebody's idiot nephew.

The security guard gazed past Dylan and asked, "You're it? Where's the rest of the Calvary?"

"I'm it," Dylan said and looked away from him and toward the front door, then took a step back and swept his gaze up and across the entire house. It was a three-story home, or maybe two stories with a finished attic from the pitch of the roof line. All the windows were pitch black, including the dormers. No sign of life, and the house was massive. *More of a mansion than the usual lake houses,* Dylan thought. It would be very enticing to his burglars; the entire house screamed of expensive toys inside.

The van was parked just before a large portico held up by ornate white pillars. The elaborate circular roof created an expansive space for their guests to disembark without consequence whatever the weather. *Old school riches,* thought Dylan. The darkened space of the deep porch would be perfect for someone breaking into the house who did not want to be seen.

Sculpted shrubbery lined the walls of the entire first story which would have hampered entry through one of the windows. They probably had a key like at the other houses but were not aware of an alarm. That thought helped him move the security guard even further down his list of suspects. Dylan shook his head. It was going to take forever to clear the place, but he still wanted to do it alone and he hoped this clown didn't suddenly want to imitate law enforcement. He didn't need some bungling rent-a-cop stumbling on whoever set off the alarm, that is if it wasn't him doing an inside job. If it was a couple of trigger happy nervous kids, and these break-ins felt like delinquent teens, anything could happen.

Dylan looked back at the caretaker and said, "You reported that a silent alarm went off?" The caretaker smirked and held up his I-Pad so that Dylan could see an app beeping an alarm. "That's it? That's the alarm?" Dylan asked.

"Yeah, what did you expect? This ain't the big city, bro," the caretaker said then snorted something that vaguely resembled a laugh.

"Right," Dylan said, then added, "Are there any security cameras?"

The man laughed and said, "Uh, no."

Dylan rubbed his forehead, nodded at the man and said, "Okay, uh, why don't you stay here in case someone comes out and I'll check the house."

"Yeah, sounds right," the security guard said, and then handed Dylan a key. He lit up another cigarette and leaned back in his seat. The village idiot had already erased his presence.

Dylan wasn't through with him, yet, though. He glanced at the nametag on the front of the blue jumpsuit and said, "Roger, is there a section of the house that has a lot of electronics? That's what my guys seem to go for."

A slight turn of his head as he said, "Hey, how'd you know my name?" Dylan pointed at the man's name tag and Roger said, "Oh, right, well, uh, the entire third floor is a righteous playroom full of shit: pinball machines, a pool table, big flat screen TV, X-box. It's sweet. That what you mean?"

Righteous? thought Dylan as he mentally adjusted the caretakers age and wondered if he still lived in his mother's basement. *Unless he is a fabulous actor, I can take him off the suspect list.* "Yes, Roger, that's what I meant," Dylan said. He patted the side of the van door and continued with, "Stay put and I'll let you know what I find."

"Roger that, man," the caretaker said, and then a strange sound exploded from the van. At first Dylan didn't recognize the noise, but then he realized that although it sounded like a barking seal, it was a laugh. He should record it; he could make a fortune selling it to an animated sitcom. "Roger that, hey, pretty good, huh? Roger being my name and all," the moron said.

Dylan turned and headed for the front door. He quickened his step, so that Roger the caretaker couldn't see his eye roll, but honestly, he could not have stopped it even if he had still been facing the man. The guy was a total tool.

Dylan forgot the inept security guard as soon as he stepped under the massive portico. His focus turned solely to his prey. *Damn, he wanted, correction, he needed to catch the little bastards in the act.* He cringed when his footsteps echoed in the cavernous stone entrance as he crossed the extensive flagstone floor. Once he reached the heavy double wooden front doors, Dylan gripped the brass door handle and it turned easily, so he tucked the key away and pushed the door open. He stepped into the front hall and eased the door closed, then gripped his flashlight and pulled out his gun.

The house appeared to be even more massive than it looked from the outside—and it was quiet; too quiet. No running feet or muffled cries, so they were either gone, *please no*, or they couldn't hear his entry into this mega mansion.

Dylan shook his head and thought, *Please, please let this be my guys, and let them still be here.* If they went for the electronic toys just like they did at all the previous locations, he would have them trapped on the third floor. He flashed his light up the duel staircases and hoped the third floor only had one entrance and exit.

He eased up the staircase on the right ignoring the first floor. He chose to follow the caretaker's information about the game room. It was a gamble, especially coming from such an unreliable source, but if they were on the first floor when their cars pulled into the driveway, they were most likely gone anyway.

On the second floor he moved down the hallway with only cursory glances into the empty bedrooms. At the end of the hallway he spotted the attic stairs and felt his pulse quicken. Unless he completely missed another hidden staircase, this was it. He eased up the stairs grateful for the plush carpeting covering each step.

He could hear them before he got within a few feet of the open playroom door. They were calling to each other and whooping and laughing in the way a couple of teenage boys would do if they had on noise cancelling headphones and were deep into the action of a game. *No wonder they didn't hear me come in,* he thought and nodded as the movie, *Ready Player One*, flashed through Dylan's mind.

He spent too many Saturdays with his nephews not to recognize those sounds. The voices seemed young; maybe high school age, or even younger. *Damn,* he thought. He hoped this didn't turn sour. He really didn't want to shoot a kid. He kept his gun out but unhooked the strap that held his taser.

Dylan headed into the playroom without any real fear of being heard. He pointed his flashlight at the floor and glanced around at the game tables only half covered by sheets until his eyes rested on his quarry. At the end of the room a flat screen television that took up about half the wall was lit up with flashes of carnage and guns blasting creatures crawling all over a dystopian landscape. No sound other than the kids uncensored joy as they annihilated another zombie. A smile as he felt his arms relax. *They are just kids.* It was what he expected, but he still needed to be cautious. Kids could be deadly sometimes. That was being played out in the news much too often these days, and after Kate, he was always braced for the unexpected.

A glance to either side of the room and he spotted the light cancelling curtains. No wonder he couldn't see any activity in the house from outside. He moved forward a few steps, but the boys were still deeply rooted into their game. "Hey," he called, but there was no reaction, so he eased even closer until he was almost on top of them and shouted, "Police!" Still nothing, so he shined his flashlight back and forth across the television screen.

This time the reaction was immediate. They both jumped up and swiveled toward him with their headphones still tethering them to the game, then the shorter one stuck both hands in the air and the other one, the bigger of the two kids, started crying as a large wet spot spread across his pants. Dylan shook his head. *Damn fool kids.*

***

Autumn headed straight into the kitchen and set her take out container on the counter as she grabbed utensils and a paper towel. She was a little ticked at herself for not taking her own container, but she had not expected to bring the meal home. She hated Styrofoam containers and what they did to landfills. She shrugged, and took it all, along with a large glass of water, and settled at the dining room table.

It was getting late and she was still hungry, so she began to eat the pasta without heating it up. It was still delicious. She felt a little barbaric feasting on the cold pasta while it was still in the takeout container, but then she shrugged, at least she was sitting at the dining room table and not standing at the kitchen sink wolfing it down. "I'm not an animal after all," she mumbled with a full mouth then chuckled and kept eating.

Sadie sat beside her watching every bite she took, so Autumn said in a stern voice, "No, Sadie, this is momma's food." The dog hung her head and moved over to the fireplace, turned around three times and then snuggled into her bed. Autumn felt her heart tighten but she knew the pasta would not be good for her canine companion.

After she finished her food, she headed for the ice chest and a beer, then took her place at the kitchen window as she thought, *I really need to shop for a refrigerator. Maybe something big with pull out drawers, an ice and water dispenser on the front, oh, and in stainless steel. Now that will look as out of place in this kitchen as pearls on a pig.* As the expression floated through her thoughts she grinned; it was something her grandmother said all the time. *Funny, grandma Aisling has not crossed my mind in such a long time.* Maybe this place was going to be good for her after all. She certainly wanted to think of more good memories and push the recent ones into the forgotten corners of her mind. Autumn could be good at forgetting if she really tried.

The lake was calm and barely visible through the window above the sink. *No stars or moon tonight, only clouds and fog,* she thought. The big white house across the lake was shrouded in darkness and swirling gray fog as if it wore a giant cloak, but she thought about the strange spark of light coming from the lower level curtained window and wondered again what it was.

It could be anything, but the house was supposed to be unoccupied, so it bothered her to see movement. Her neighbors, Pat and Terri, told her no one was living there, and it was vacant for over a year, so why the glint of light through the curtains?

She supposed the real estate agent could be showing it and simply rustled the curtains, but what if it was something more ominous? Maybe it was the burglars Dylan was hunting? Her eyes narrowed as she tried to see through the fog, but if anything, the night was enveloping the house even more.

Dylan seemed to think teens were responsible for the break-ins. Autumn took another cold sip of her beer and then paused as a chill moved up her back. Was it possible the teens behind the break-ins were also the ones playing tricks on her with the teddy bear and flowers? The chill evaporated, and she felt her face grow hot, but she tried to push the bubbling anger away.

If some bored teens were messing with the new lady, so what? But still, she really would like to catch the little monsters and give them a scare right back. *Nothing like a little taste of their own medicine.* Another one of Grandma Aisling's sayings.

Maybe she would take a walk around the lake in the morning when it was sunny and get a closer look at the house. She walked the distance around the finger portion of the lake for exercise a couple of times, but she was concentrating on her walk and not paying a lot of attention to the big white house.

Admittedly, the house stood out from the other houses in her section of the lake. It's size and age alone set it apart from the newer and smaller homes. She gazed at it as it rose out of the fog and the white wood siding looked almost gray in the night. Her imagination was probably feeding her mood, but the house looked like something out of a Stephen King novel with its current setting.

It would be a nice walk on the quiet, tree lined street. Maybe it would be a good route to take Sadie for a longer stroll. She leaned back and smiled as another idea formed. *Maybe it is a good time to try out my new kayak and paddle over.* The house had a dock area where she could tie up and the window in question was just up the hill from the shore line. Since the house was vacant, there was no one to care.

Autumn finished her beer and tossed the bottle into her recycling bin before checking the locks again, and then she headed up the stairs to her bedroom. She had already taken Sadie out for her nightly trip to relieve herself, so the dog jumped up from her bed by the fireplace and kept pace with her while the cats followed at a discreet distance.

Ying and Yang had to seem independent of the nightly parade to bed; as if the trip was solely their idea. Not Sadie, though, she seemed happy to be clumped in with a group. *Her new pack.* Autumn chuckled, then sobered as she wondered absently if Jan Miller had had a nightly routine that she and Sadie adhered to, and then her thoughts turned darker. *What happened to her?* She wondered if she would ever find out or if it would forever remain a mystery. Autumn looked at Sadie, sighed and then began to get ready for bed.

As she settled under the covers and picked up a book, the strange dream she had earlier while she was in the bath snaked into her thoughts. She absently stroked Ying as she tried to remember what the dream was all about. She knew there was something about a chain around her ankle and she had felt incredibly trapped. Like most dreams, or at least what she could remember of them after they faded, it was more of a jumble of feelings than concrete actions. She knew the dream made her feel panicked and left her with a strong desire to run, but that was about it. What she was certain of, was that she did not want to dream it again, much like the closet dream. *What is with all these strange nightmares?* Autumn thought. She did not remember ever being prone to them before.

Autumn shook her head and leaned over and exchanged the suspenseful book she first picked up for a historical biography. She enjoyed her kindle when she traveled, but she liked the feel of a book with paper and always kept several eclectic books on her bedside table so that she could read to suit her mood. Right now, she wanted something engaging, but completely vanilla. One chapter in and she yawned. *Maybe not engaging, but certainly vanilla. The perfect choice,* she thought.

Chapter 16

Dylan hung up the phone. He closed his eyes and rested his forehead on the stack of files on his desk. *I need sleep*, he thought. The conversation with Madge Brody was every bit as unpleasant as he anticipated and sucked up the last of his energy. He leaned back and opened his eyes as he gazed at the ceiling and mumbled, "Damn kids."

Josh's mother was the lake's local real estate agent. She found his rental for him when he relocated from Chicago, so he knew her well. Almost too well. When she found out Dylan was single, she flirted openly with him, and when he didn't respond, she asked him out. He flinched and blushed when he remembered making it abundantly clear that he was not interested. He could have handled the rebuke a lot better than he did and would have to be gentle with the interrogation. Dylan hated feeling like he was a total ass to someone and then needing to *play nice* to make up for it. That was happening much too often lately.

Josh's mom handled almost all the Lake Phillips property needs, so now that Dylan knew it was her kid it made sense that the break-ins occurred only in vacant houses. He mentally kicked himself for not checking out more people who would have access to that information. It took thinking about the security service moron last night before he went down that avenue of thought. *Not good.*

Dylan's first assumption was that the burglars used surveillance to locate empty houses, but simple, basic police work would have given him Josh's name and might have prevented most of this. Since he suspected teenagers, it wouldn't be much of a leap to look at the family of people in the lake with occupancy information.

Dylan clearly had not been the best at his job since he lost his partner and that needed to change. *I need to change*, he thought. It wasn't Lake Phillips fault his partner died before his eyes and they deserved better policing for their community. A smile as he thought, *My community.*

The access to residential occupancy might be valuable information for young Josh, but it was about to spell disaster for his mother's career. This could destroy the trust the community placed in her to protect their information. Small town connections were strong, but with something this invasive, folks were probably going to be distancing themselves from her. As expected, after he told Madge he had her son in custody and why, she voiced disbelief, then outrage, then tears.

Although he called Timmy's parents first, Madge was going to beat them to the station because both of his parents had to get away from their jobs and Madge was at home working. He told himself he wanted Timmy's folks to come in as quickly as possible since the kid couldn't seem to stop blubbering, but Dylan knew his real reason. He was stalling before he had to see Madge Brody. He had already asked for a search warrant, maybe he should send Wilson to serve it and escort her to the station. It would buy him a little more time. *McAlister, you are such a coward*, he thought.

He was almost feeling sorry for the kids. *Almost.* The pair caused him, and everyone else in Lake Phillips, a lot of grief with their youthful crime spree. The real pity he felt was for their parents. Caught between the love of your kid and being furious with them was not an easy place to be. He knew what it was like, but from the other end. With six siblings and a big Irish family, one of his brothers, sisters or cousins was always in hot water.

He stretched, yawned and blinked several times. The long night was about to turn into a long day. *Stupid kids.* They not only let their parents and the community down, but they spoiled his date with Autumn. He grinned as he thought about her. He couldn't help it.

He not only surprised Autumn when he asked her to consider it a date, he surprised himself. He had no idea the statement was going to come out of his mouth until it did, but she accepted, so his blundering paid off. *Life is still worth taking chances*, he thought.

Honestly, he wasn't sure how he felt about dating again, but, well, maybe it was okay, and there was something about the redhead that kept her popping up in his thoughts. She was bullheaded, argumentative, and fiercely independent. She had even more baggage to deal with than he did, but, she made him smile again, and that was something.

He turned toward the front of the office and called to the receptionist, "Lucy, could you please let me know when their parents get in?" The woman nodded her gray head without looking up. The silver hair shaped in a clean bowl cut didn't move with the nod. Dylan stared at her and thought, *her hair fits her like a skull cap. Yep, just like Mrs. Cox.* Maybe the fear he still held of his former teacher's wrath was what kept him from warming up to Lucy. He would have to make more of an effort with the receptionist since she was a Lake Phillips fixture. She was one of the founders of the community and would probably work at the police department in some capacity for the rest of her life.

Dylan glanced at the hallway leading to the cells. He wasn't allowed to talk to the teens until their parents got to the station and he really wanted to interrogate the little gangsters. He sat for a moment as he read through the burglary files again. The sheer number of items that these two took was going to add up. It might become grand theft, and if so, these kids were looking at some serious consequences.

"Stupid kids," Dylan mumbled, then closed the files and picked up his cell phone. A glance at Lucy and Dylan headed for the break room. He had a sudden urge to reach out to Autumn and he didn't want the whole town to know they were seeing each other, although, around here, the town probably knew it was happening before they did.

He paused in the hallway and turned back toward the reception area and called, "Getting some coffee, can I get you a cup?" The gray head rose, and Lucy turned watery blue eyes in his direction. A slight negative shake of her head then she looked down again. But as Dylan turned toward the break room he smiled. He could swear there was a tiny upward curve to her lips which he had not seen since he started with the Lake Phillips PD. Dylan's smile turned into a grin as he headed down the hallway.

***

Autumn glanced at her cell phone, then swiped green to answer as she said, "Good morning, Dylan."

"Hi, how are you this morning?"

She noticed a flutter in her chest with the soft-spoken words and mentally admonished herself. Autumn rose from the table and carried her empty cereal bowl into the kitchen and placed it in the sink. "I'm good. I just finished breakfast. Did you catch your guys?" she said as she placed her mug under the spigot of her single cup coffee maker and slipped in another coffee pod, then pushed the button and watched it flow into the cup. She took a deep breath; the smell of the dark brew was intoxicating. Coffee in the morning headed the top of her list for her favorite things in life.

"I did, but it was two teenage boys, so because they are under age, I have to wait for their parents to get here so that I can talk to them."

"Oh, man, I bet you are exhausted. Those kids are going to be in so much trouble with their folks," she replied.

"I am tired, but I hope to catch a nap later after all this is settled. You're right about them being in trouble; you should have heard the reaction when I called their parents, and they still have no idea how much. The amount of stuff they took might add up to grand theft. Dumb kids."

"That's too bad." She grabbed her full mug and headed to the kitchen window. She took a sip and enjoyed the warm, slightly bitter taste as it rolled over her tongue.

The window framed an idyllic picture of the lake. The sun was bouncing off the water sending sparks of light dancing up into the sky. Autumn watched a kayak glide over the smooth surface with long V shaped waves floating in its wake as it moved past her property and headed toward the larger part of the lake. Just as the lone kayaker disappeared, she caught movement from the big white house opposite her.

Autumn leaned forward and gazed at the downstairs window that caught her eye. It happened again; a slight flutter of the curtain, then nothing. No hint of light this time, but the deep porch was shaded from the sun and there didn't appear to be an interior light on. Autumn frowned and set her cup on the counter as she leaned closer to the window and thought, *What's up with that? Why do I keep seeing movement in an empty house?*

Maybe it was simply someone showing the place or cleaning it, or perhaps someone moved in and her intel was out of date. She squinted and stared across the lake. *But what if it is some kid taking advantage of the vacant house? Maybe Dylan's teen boys were part of a gang of teens, and he only has two of them, and what if it's the same kids who left that box and then broke in my house?*

She realized Dylan was talking and her thoughts were blocking her ability to listen to what he was saying, so she said, "Sorry, I missed that, could you say it again?"

His voice sounded in her ear as he began talking about making dinner up to her, but Autumn kept her eyes glued to the house as she tried to listen to him and process what he was saying. But then he said, "Oh, I hear someone out front and they sound angry. Better go, I think this may be one of the kid's parents."

"Oh, Okay, good luck--but, uh, Dylan, are you sure you have all of them in custody?" she asked. She paused a moment as she leaned closer to the window and then said, "I mean the kids? Could there be more teens involved?"

"I won't know any details until I can talk to the little monsters in person. I'll let you know as soon as I am through with the interrogations---Might be a while, though."

"Sure, sure, okay; go take care of them. Bye, Dylan," She said as she disconnected the call and shoved her phone into the back pocket of her jeans. She gave the white house her full attention, but the curtains remained closed and without a single flutter. "I might be over thinking this, but still, I believe it's time to investigate," she mumbled, but as she started to turn from the window her eyes landed on her new kayak lying upside down in the yard by her dock and she remembered her idea from the previous night. She smiled. *Perfect.*

Autumn took Sadie out for a quick trip around the yard. After the dog was back in the house, she grabbed her life vest and keys before she glanced at the almost full coffee mug, shrugged, and kept going. *I love my coffee, but my curiosity needs answering. I am tired of all this not knowing,* she thought as she headed for the back door.

Sadie followed her closely and planted herself close to the door as she stared unblinking at Autumn. A hand on the door knob made the dog whine and ease forward, so Autumn smiled at her and said, "Not this time girl, momma needs to explore on her own," and she slipped out of the door and shut it behind herself.

As Autumn headed down the steps she could hear the dog barking. She stopped and looked back at the house, then shook her head and continued down to her dock. This exploration would be far better without a curious and noisy dog by her side, and the kayak would work for her purposes much better than a walk.

The kayak would be a stealthier approach to the big white house and it would be much faster than if she was on a walk around the lakes horseshoe finger. She could have driven but pulling up in front of the house would alert anyone who was inside.

With the water approach, she could tie up at the houses' massive dock and head up to the back door from the lake. The curtain movement and glint were at the basement level, so arriving from the water would make it appear a more natural starting place instead of slipping around from the front of the house without ringing the front bell.

If she indeed had a new neighbor, perhaps they might invite her in and they could chat. The worst thing she thought would happen was that they might think she was a nosey neighbor. Autumn decided she could live with that.

If the house was empty, and the vibes she was getting from the secretive flutters were what she suspected, maybe she could catch the little creeps who were part of this juvenile crime spree. She had her cell, so she would call Dylan to come get them, but only after she asked them why the hell they left that awful teddy bear on her bed. It was a win, win as far as she could tell. At the very least, maybe she could see how visible her house was from across the lake.

Autumn flipped the kayak over and pulled it down to the water and began to put on her life vest. She leaned back and took a deep breath. Fall had to be her favorite time of year. Light jackets and jeans before the turtle necks and boots came out. Shorts and flip flops were great, but she did love the transition months to winter. She still found it ironic that she was named the same as the season she loved so much, even with her mother's explanation, and she toyed with the idea of putting it into one of her songs. *Maybe someday*, she thought.

Autumn eased her kayak into the water and tied it to her bulkhead. She climbed into the kayak, grabbed the paddle and untied the ropes. As she pushed off and slid forward beside her dock, she dipped the paddle into the water and used it to move out toward the center of the lake. She felt a little thrill as she surged forward and was happy she chose the water over a walk on the road.

The street in front of Autumn's property encircled the entire lake and smaller roads branched off it and led to other neighborhoods. This narrow end of the large lake ended in a horseshoe curve with a couple of triangular properties that were also lake front. Autumn lived on one side of the horseshoe and the big white house was on the other side.

As she glided over the smooth surface she gazed to her left at the houses between her cabin and the big white house. She was amazed at how different they looked from a water perspective.

From the street side, most appeared to be one story and small, but from the back view, she could see that many of them dropped down their sloped yards into multiple stories. She could only imagine the hidden rooms inside, and all the windows must have great water views.

The trip walking around the lake would have taken about 20 or 30 minutes even at a brisk pace. She could cut that in half by kayaking. The roads surrounding the lake were two-lane streets with no sidewalks or easement. Instead, they were bordered by leaf covered drainage ditches that meant certain death for a car's axel if you were unlucky enough to drop a tire off the road into one.

The lake roads were filled with blind corners, making a walker vulnerable to vehicles, so you had to be cautious and slow, although there were very few cars at this time of day. Running would have gotten her there about as quick as kayaking, but she wasn't a runner. Running gave her shin splints and made everything hurt, but she could walk forever.

Autumn took another deep breath and she could smell pine in the cool breeze that swept across the water. She smiled and then gazed at the heavily forested lots surrounding the lake. There were several evergreens, but the rest of the trees held leaves that were becoming radiant with a full collage of color. Autumn loved the sound of the crunching leaves under her tennis shoes when she walked the road, but she was on a mission and not looking for a simple brisk morning walk. Besides, the maiden voyage of her kayak was proving to be exhilarating.

She felt the muscles in her shoulders and back engage as she increased her paddling motion and the kayak surged forward at an intoxicating speed across the glassy surface. As she got past the center of the lake a group of ducks that were heading her way abruptly changed direction and their leader skidded them toward deeper water with some loud squawks. "Sorry, guys," she called to them as she sped closer to her target.

Autumn used her paddle to slow almost to a stop once she got within reach of the opposite shore and floated for a moment as she scanned the house and the yard leading up to it. "Wow," she mumbled. The place was a sprawling Victorian style complete with turrets, multiple porches and decks, a large extended dock, and a boat house with a lift. It was an older house, maybe turn of the century, but well maintained and it looked like it had a fresh coat of white paint.

She decided to head around the main dock toward a small sandy beach. The owners must have had several trucks bring in all the pristine looking sand to form such a natural looking beach. It would be the perfect place to leave her kayak and would also make for a quick get-a-way if she needed to leave in a hurry.

Autumn paddled past the main section of the dock and the boat house which had a covered speed boat cradled in the boat lift. Two kayaks were tethered to a ladder on the dock, and there was even a canoe turned upside down on the beach. *These folks like their water toys,* she thought as she hit the beach with the nose of her kayak and then scooted forward until it was grounded into the sand. She stepped out of the kayak and pulled it the rest of the way out of the water, then she turned it around until the nose was pointed toward the lake.

She stood in the sand and her eyes followed the manicured lawn beyond the beach up to the house as she examined the windows and French doors. The curtains were still drawn, but she could see a slight opening on the basement level. She squinted. There was an object about half way up the window. It was something shiny and metallic. *Perhaps my glint of light?* she thought. But, as hard as she stared, she was still too far away to tell what it was.

Autumn turned and gazed back across the lake. She found herself looking directly at the back of her house. It was an odd feeling; almost like looking at herself through someone else's eyes. There was enough distance across the lake that she could not see into her windows, but as expected, it was a completely unobstructed view.

She held up her phone and pulled up the camera app. As she gazed through the camera's eye, she used her fingers to draw her house closer, and there was her big plate glass window with Sadie's face staring out. She felt a sudden chill and was very glad she had gotten curtains after all. She pocketed her phone again and turned around to look at the big white Victorian rambler.

Her head swiveled around the backyard and then back toward the water. No one was on the lake, and she couldn't see the neighboring houses because of the dense trees, so she walked up the hill until she was standing on the lawn in front of the concrete patio at the walkout basement level.

The basement patio was sheltered by a second story deck, but it sat at just the right angle to still get some sunlight for a small portion of the day. Now that she was so close, it was easy to see the round object that had caused her glint.

Autumn placed her hands on her hips and frowned. The tip of a silver metallic telescope poked through the curtains. She turned and gazed over her shoulder, then back at the window. The telescope appeared to be aimed directly at her house instead of at the stars. Her frown deepened, and she could feel a familiar fire rise from her belly up to her face.

With the basement windows shaded by the second story deck, the telescope could only be used to view across the lake. If they were star gazing, it would be on a higher level of the house. Perhaps they liked watching the swans and geese on the water, but Autumn doubted it. The water or sky could be observed from the second or third story, where the basement level revealed only her house and the lake. Also, tucked away like that, it was a little too secretive to be a normal placement.

Autumn stomped up to the back door before she could change her mind. Her anger was driving her feet, but she didn't even try to contain it. Logic told her the occurrences from the last few days were helping to fuel the rage she felt, but she was too furious to allow her mind to slow her down.

A rap of her knuckles on the curtain shrouded glass door drew no response, so she pounded harder with the side of her fist and the door pushed opened a crack. Autumn blinked. *Did the doorknob turn before the door pushed open? No way,* she thought, then placed her tennis shoe against the bottom of the door and pushed harder. The door swung inward, but she couldn't see anyone inside the darkened room.

"Hello? Anyone home?" She called, but only silence greeted her. She took a deep breath and her shoulders slumped. As her anger dissipated slightly, a chill moved up her spine as she had a flash of the door opening at Jan Miller's house. She pursed her lips, then shrugged and backed up a step as she gazed at the open door.

I should close this door and go—Anything else would be considered trespassing and make me as bad as those teens. I can call the real estate agent and talk to her —or Dylan, he would know what to do, Autumn thought, then sighed and stepped forward to reach for the door knob to pull it closed, but as she did, an interior wall covered in photos caught her eye. "What tha—" she mumbled and blinked again.

The room was dark but the sunlight from the open door gave her just enough light to see the gallery of pictures. Her eyes widened. *Is that me?* she thought as her mouth fell open and she edged in another step. Her hand remained lightly resting on the doorknob, but her complete attention was laser focused on the pictures and she took one more step forward.

Autumn stood very still and barely breathed as she stared toward the wall. She couldn't see who was in most of the pictures, they were too small, and it was too dim, but one of them, an 8 x 11 shot, was easy to make out. It was one of her publicity shots she took at a studio in Nashville. *What is going on here?* she thought as a jumble of questions fought with each other in her mind. Her head turned to the window and the telescope was in full view. Her heart began pounding and she broke out in a sweat.

A voice behind the door said, "Hello, Michelle."

She jumped and whirled toward the voice. A man; a very tall and thin man, stood almost motionless in the shadows behind the door watching her. Sky blue eyes and short blond hair with a childlike face. *Where had she seen that face? Oh, crap, it was the guy in the back at Cowboys the night of Richard's tribute.* Her ears began to ring, and her hands felt wet as realization swept over her. He was the adult version of the boy in her nightmare. "Uh, sorry," she said as her mind screamed, *You idiot, you walked right into this…*

As Autumn edged backwards toward the open door, the doorknob flew out of her hand as he shoved the door closed with a bang.

"I have waited so long for this, Michelle," he said as he moved closer until he towered above her. His eyes played over her face. "You haven't changed at all."

"My name isn't Michelle and I have to go," Autumn said as she reached for the door knob again, but before she could grasp it he sprang forward and wrapped one arm around her waist and the other around her arms. *How does someone that tall and gangly move so fast,* was her first thought, but her second was, *I'm screwed.* She felt like a bug caught in a spider web with the long-legged spider wrapping around her.

"Sorry, but I can't let you do that, Michelle," he said as one of his arms slipped up and across her neck and she began to struggle for air. She clawed at his arm and squirmed as hard as she could. A vision of Richard tied to a chair with fourteen stab wounds and blood everywhere played through her thoughts, so she fought with everything she had, but then the world went black.

Chapter 17

Dylan studied Josh and his mother as they sat across the desk from him. The tension between them felt like a balloon about to burst. He was worried about Madge Brody. Her face was bright red, and she stared straight ahead without a glance in her son's direction. The boy hung his head, but would occasionally glance at his mother, then he would drop his head again to stare at his hands.

The kid's hands were on the table in front of him and he kept picking at his cuticles. *Pick, pick, pick.* Dylan noticed a speck of blood on his right thumb which the boy wiped on his shorts, then the hands went back to the table and it started again. Mom's hand shot out and pulled Josh's hands apart without turning her head or looking at him.

Dylan pulled his eyes away from the train wreck and cleared his throat. He reached into the file box by his feet and then spread several plastic evidences bags across the table. They were filled with stolen items and a wad of cash from the kid's room. He didn't need to ask Wilson to serve the warrant and search the Brody house, she volunteered. At least it had delayed his face to face with Madge a little longer.

Dylan probably should have gone to the Brody house himself. He could only imagine how officer Wilson handled it, but honestly, he simply couldn't do it. Seeing Madge Brody now, though, he regretted his decision. Her world was ripped apart and she had to act professional in an impossible situation with no support.

Being a single mother was tough enough, but having your kid get in deep with the law and have your livelihood threatened at the same time, was a little too much for anyone to handle. Then there was the tension between Dylan and Madge after the fiasco flirtation. *As much as I wanted to catch these guys, I do not want to be here,* Dylan thought. He glared at Josh but seeing how miserable the boy was made him soften his gaze.

Madge cleared her throat and finally made eye contact with Dylan as she said in a voice tight with anger, "Dylan, uh, officer McAlister, I'm sure this is some sort of misunderstanding. My boy would never betray the confidence my clients to do something like this. It must be that other boy, Timmy, who isn't the brightest bulb in the box, if you get my meaning. He must have given this stuff to my Josh." Dylan noticed her hands were shaking as she reached for the water bottle in front of her and took a long gulp.

Josh's jaw dropped, and he mumbled, "No, mom, it wasn't like that…"

She held up one hand without turning her head toward her son as she set the water bottle down and continued with, "Seriously, my boy would not do this." Her mouth sagged into a deep frown and her shoulders drooped as she whispered, "He couldn't have…"

"I'm so sorry, mom, really, I am." The kid looked like he might start crying. "It wasn't Timmy; it was my idea."

Geeze, these crazy kids are done for. The amount of stuff they took is going to add up to some serious jail time, Dylan thought, but he said, "Mrs. Brody, both boys were caught in the act and Josh had a room full of stolen goods. They are equally in trouble here; real trouble. Their age will help a little, but they are old enough to do some jail time; possibly a lot of jail time. I suggest you get a good lawyer before we go any further with this and I am going to advise Timmy's parents to do the same."

Her face went from red to the color of paper and she turned to her son and said, "What have you done, Josh? What have you done?" Then they both began to cry.

Dylan pushed his chair back and stood. He said, "Uh, I'll give you a minute," as he pushed a box of tissues toward them and headed out of the room.

Back at his desk, he retrieved his cell phone and checked his messages, but there was nothing. He called and texted her several times, but it kept going directly to voicemail and she wasn't responding to his texts. Maybe she was napping or working on her music and the phone was off. He texted her a simple, "Call me,"-Dylan, then he headed toward the break room for more coffee.

He was drinking too much coffee, especially the strong station house brew, but with no sleep, and worrying about these boys, and now wondering why Autumn was avoiding him, he needed the sludge.

Dylan rolled his eyes. Why had he sent that last text? He didn't want Autumn to think he was desperate, but she had asked him for an update, so why wasn't she checking in? He should have simply waited for her to text him. The last thing she needed was more pressure. *Damn,* he thought as he wished he could pull the text back out of cyber space.

Autumn's time since she got to Lake Phillips had been one nightmare after another, so he didn't want to be the source of more stress. Besides, if he tried too hard in the beginning it would scare her off. *Hell, I will scare myself off if I feel too much too soon, or if I feel rejection this early.*

He shoved the phone into his pocket and tried to turn his thoughts back to the burglaries, but thoughts about the case were just as bad. He wished he could come up with a solution that would keep the young boys out of jail, but the weight of what they stole went far beyond community service and a slap on the wrist. Their entire future was about to change.

Officer Wilson came into the break room and it broke his train of thought. He nodded at her and realized he was glad to see her for once, but it was fleeting when he saw her expression; she looked like she just won the jackpot on a slot machine. She was practically glowing. "Hey, I moved Timmy's parents into the meeting room since you have Josh and his mom in the interrogation room." She leaned against the counter and smirked as she said, "That Timmy kid can't quit crying and he smells like piss."

Dylan frowned; the woman was without empathy as far as he could tell, and she was acting like a puffed-up little dictator. The *interrogation room* was basically an extra office for the highway patrol when they stopped in, or any other traveling law enforcement. He liked seeing eagerness in newly minted officers, but Wilson's attitude bordered on cruelty, and that was never good in law enforcement. With the power of the badge came responsibility. He thought of several retorts, but instead he said, "Thanks."

She nodded and said, "I logged the stuff from his house and it's in the box on your desk. Quite a haul when you add it to Josh's loot." She tucked her hands in her pockets and winked.

"Okay, got it," Dylan said, then headed toward his desk to go through the items.

Lucy walked up to him as he was examining the evidence bags and said, "Mrs. Brody is asking to speak with you again."

He looked up and noticed Lucy appeared more worried than severe for once, and he realized she probably knew both the boys and their parents. "Okay, I'll be right there, Lucy," he said. Dylan pushed the box aside and his shoulders sagged as he thought, *Now comes the begging, but there isn't much I can do for them at this point.*

As Dylan entered the office where he left the mother and son, he immediately felt a change, but not the one he expected. Josh was sitting up straight and Madge Brody had her arm draped around his chair.

"My Josh has some information we would like to trade for leniency," Madge said as she stuck out her chin. This was more like the woman who he witnessed in negotiating his lease. She looked Dylan in the eye and her color was back to normal. He left the room to a couple of basket cases and came back to a different family. This family was at ease and in control.

Dylan tilted his head to one side and asked her, "What sort of information?"

"Information of a more serious crime," she said as she shifted to an even straighter posture.

Dylan blocked the sigh he felt coming and asked, "Mrs. Brody, what sort of crime? What are you talking about?"

"Please, call me Madge," she said. "I can't give you the details until we have a guarantee you will give my Josh a break, but he knows the location of evidence of a much more serious crime. Much worse than a couple of misguided boys taking a few items; I am talking about a possible murder."

"*What?*" Dylan asked. He sat across from them and leaned forward as he pinned Josh against his chair with his glare. "What did you see, Josh? Was it at one of the houses you broke in to? Which one?"

Josh swallowed hard and dropped his eyes, but it was his mother who answered Dylan. "Uh, we would like that lawyer you were suggesting first, officer McAlister. This is important, but we need to have some protection," she said as her shoulders went back, and the chin went even higher.

Josh's head popped up and he looked at his mother as he said, "Timmy, too, mom. He wanted to tell all along, so he has to get the break, also."

Madge Brody frowned at her son, sighed, and nodded, then looked at Dylan and said, "You heard him."

"I'll get you your lawyer, but you need to be forthcoming if anyone is in imminent danger." He turned to her and said, "If he saw something that he should have reported and didn't, he could be in even more trouble than he is now."

The mother looked at her son and he gave a quick shake of his head. She turned to Dylan and said, "We believe this crime to have already occurred, but the sooner you get a lawyer for us to speak with, the better."

***

Autumn awoke with a start. She was lying on a cot in a windowless room that wasn't much bigger than a walk-in closet. She sat up and felt something heavy around her ankle. She glanced down and gasped when she saw it was a chain with large metal links. *Oh, my god, it's just like my dream,* she thought.

She took a deep breath and gazed around the room as she examined every inch of the space. It didn't take long because there wasn't much to see. She shivered. This all felt very familiar for some reason. Her eyes widened, and she jerked around and checked her back pocket, but her cell phone was gone.

She squeezed her eyes shut and took another deep breath, then opened them and tried to examine the space using logic instead of fear. Her cot was shoved tightly into the corner of the room, directly across from the door. The door itself was odd. It was flush with the wall and had no knob or lock, so she assumed it could only be opened from the outside. The entire room had white padding covering the walls and ceiling. Another shiver as she thought, *Soundproofing.* It might be possible to rip the padding from the walls, but she would most likely be discovered long before she was able to get very far.

There was a sink in the opposite corner from the cot and what appeared to be a camp toilet beside it. *Lovely*, she thought. A bedside table held a lamp that cast a soft light around the space and an unopened bottle of water. She touched the lamp and gave it a gentle push. It was glued or bolted to the table. Autumn frowned. *He really thought of everything.*

The chain on her ankle slinked across the room and was attached to an iron bar beside the door. The lock holding the ends of the chain together was odd looking; it was a combination lock, but with letters instead of numbers and it had 8 digits instead of the usual 4 or 5. Autumn rubbed her temples and thought, *I am so stupid! I walked right into this. My damn temper has gotten me into trouble before, but this time I've really done it.*

She looked up and examined the ceiling. A small circular air conditioning vent was above the cot, but it was much too small to fit through unless you were a cat. Above the door she spotted a tiny camera. She raised her hand toward the camera and gave it a middle finger salute, then dropped her head into her hands.

Think, Autumn, think, but her mind could only keep processing the same word over and over, *Stupid, stupid, stupid!*

Chapter 18

Dylan found himself standing at Autumn's door. He did not intend to come here. He left the station and was heading to the store to pick up some dinner, a little something from the wine section, and then head straight home. His usual night.

Ollie, his sweet little Cairn terrier, would be waiting patiently for the sound of his car pulling into the garage. Ollie had his doggie door and a tiny back yard for his potty but loved companionship. He would take the dog for a walk and then enjoy his dinner and the bottle of wine before slipping into a sweet oblivion. It was comfortable. He liked his routine and it worked for him, but instead, here he stood, miles out of his comfort zone and feeling like a fool.

It was dusk. He had not heard from Autumn since early this morning. He thought the call went well. He knew men could be clueless when it came to a women's responses, but there was nothing in the conversation that seemed like a rejection. *It's only been a day, McAlister; what were you expecting?* But the day was a long one, and difficult, and he really wanted to hear her voice.

Although he struck an agreement with the teen's new attorney, he still hadn't gotten the warrant he was waiting for. Dylan was finding that although he wanted away from city life; things moved much slower when there wasn't a plethora of judges and lawyers everywhere. Patience was not one of his virtues, so he would need to work on that if he was going to make a home here.

Dylan could take a hint as easily as the next guy, but he was out of practice with this dating thing, and he really liked Autumn, and he got the impression that she liked him as well. They both had baggage. They were both damaged. It might just work. *Not if you come on too strong or slip over into stalker territory, McAlister*, he thought as he stared at the door.

He shrugged his shoulders and knocked. *I'm here, I might as well check on her,* he thought. Wild barking came from the other side of the door and it continued uninterrupted. If Autumn was home, she would have quieted the dog. He glanced around, and noticed her pickup truck parked in its usual spot in the carport to the right of the house. His face reddened. She must be out with someone who picked her up. A glance over his shoulder. What if they came home to find him standing here like a pitiful, needy twerp.

He headed toward his car as he thought about how stupid it was for him to assume an attractive woman like her wouldn't have other men pursuing her. It could even be someone from her husband's band who wanted to *console* her now that the ex was dead. Couldn't blame them. She was special. So why did his fist clinch at the thought?

Dylan pulled his car out onto the main road, hesitated, then pulled into Pat and Terri's driveway. "What are you doing?" he mumbled, but he still cut the engine and trudged up to their house.

Pat opened the door before he could knock and said, "Dylan, what a nice surprise. Please, come in."

"Good evening, Pat. I don't want to bother you, but uh, have you seen Autumn today?"

She joined him on her porch and gazed toward Autumn's house. It wasn't visible through the trees, so she turned toward him and said, "No, I haven't. Is anything wrong?"

He took a step back and felt his face grow red again as he said, "No, nothing's wrong. I had dinner with her last night and we had to cut it short for a case that I got called in on--- I just thought I would check in with her to see if she wanted a rain check, but she doesn't seem to be home."

Pat smiled and said, "Oh, I see. Uh, I assume you called her?"

A glance toward the tree barrier and he said, "Yeah, but it went straight to voicemail, and although her truck is there, she wasn't home, so I thought she might be over here for one of your famous cocktail hours." He rocked back and forth from one foot to the other.

That brought a laugh, and then she said, "No, haven't seen her, but if I do, I'll let her know you were looking for her."

"Oh, no, uh, that's okay, Pat, no big deal," he said as he raised one hand palm up and shook it, then jammed both hands into his pockets and rocked back on his heels.

Pat leaned against the door frame and said, "The case you spoke about, was it the teen boys that were doing the break-ins? Josh and Timmy?"

Dylan dropped one foot down a step and left the other on the porch as he said, "Wow, word does travel fast around here. Yes, it was. We have them in custody."

Pat nodded and said, "Too bad. I'm glad you stopped the break-ins, but I'm sorry it was those two. It's what I heard, but I was hoping the information was wrong." She frowned and shook her head, then said, "Those two boys have been best friends since kindergarten, but they don't always make good decisions. I guess they are in for it now. I bet their parents are fit to be tied, especially Madge. I can't imagine how upset she must be."

"Yeah, it doesn't look too good for them right now, but we may be able to help them out a little. I can't discuss the details, but we are working on a warrant for something Josh is helping us with that may create some leniency for them when we can serve it. It will most likely come through by tomorrow morning. Then we'll see what happens."

Her eyebrows rose, and she said, "Intriguing. I understand completely that you can't talk about it, but I am very glad you might be able to help them. I hate to see such young lives get ruined. But, like I said, I'm glad you caught them, and that this rash of burglaries will stop. Folks were getting a little nervous."

Dylan nodded. He was relieved she didn't ask him what he meant about the warrant; he had already said too much, but he should have known she wouldn't ask. Pat was an intelligent caring woman. She may have her ear to the town gossip, but he suspected she never solicited it and she would never overstep. "Okay, well, I better get home to Ollie," he said as he started down the rest of the steps.

"Are you sure you don't want to come in? Terri will be home soon, and we can have one of those famous cocktail hours you were talking about." There was a twinkle in her eyes as she said it.

He chuckled and said, "No. I would like to take you up on that another time, but with no sleep last night, and the long day I have just had, I would most likely pass out on your couch if I had a drink, but thanks all the same."

Pat nodded, smiled, and headed back into her house as she called, "Take care, Dylan. We will make plans real soon. Maybe we can include Autumn." He cringed, nodded and kept walking to his car. He needed to get used to small town life and part of that was everyone knowing your private business.

***

Dylan finished his glass of wine and headed into his kitchen for a beer. The wine bottle was already in the recycle bin, but a beer chaser would be just about a perfect way to end the evening. He noticed his gait was slightly unsteady as he walked, but he still wanted another drink. He knew he was drinking too much and should be sleeping. He had not had any real rest, other than a short nap in his recliner, for the last 24hours, but his mind wouldn't let him sleep, it only wanted to be numb.

149

He stood at the refrigerator with the door open staring at the empty shelves as if by some magic they would suddenly fill themselves with a bounty of choices. One wilted celery stick was all it contained. *Where did that come from?* he thought as the ancient Frigidaire began to hum. The old unit hummed a lot, but when you kept the door open, it really got to jamming. The thing was probably as old as Dylan was, so he couldn't blame it for making a little noise when it had to work too hard.

He shut the door and turned and stared at his car keys hanging on the nail by the front door. "Bad idea. You should not be driving, McAlister," he said, but then he snapped his finger and put himself through the drunk driving test. He touched his nose with his index finger as he alternated with both hands, walked an imaginary line from the kitchen to the door, then shrugged and grabbed the keys. The store wasn't far, and he would head straight there and back. And he had snoozed a bit in the chair after he finished his wine.

His dog Ollie, a tiny mass of brown fur with only black eyes and a button nose showing, jumped off the couch and ran to join him, but he said, "No way, Ollie. Daddy will not let you ride with someone who might be slightly inebriated." The dog stretched then ran to grab his well-worn tennis ball and rolled it to Dylan's feet. "What? You don't think dad should be driving? I will be fine my little man and will be back soon." He headed out the door feeling a little guilty. He was even a disappointment to his sweet Ollie.

Dylan drove to the store and made his purchase, but when he pulled out of the parking lot with the case of beer resting on the back seat, he found himself turning the opposite direction from his cabin. "McAlister, you are treading on thin ice," he mumbled.

The mini mart was between his apartment and Autumn's house, so he knew where he was heading, even if he had not consciously planned to go that way. *I just want to see if she is home, then I will leave. She will never know I was there*, he thought, but deep down he knew it was a bad idea.

As he eased down Autumn's driveway he killed his lights and rolled forward. When he got close enough to the house, he braked to a complete stop and turned off his car. He leaned forward and let his eyes travel from the first story, to the second story windows. *It's completely dark.*

Dylan's head swiveled to look toward the carport. *Her truck is still here.* He leaned back in the seat and pulled out his cell phone. No little number sitting in the corner of the text message box or phone call icon. He texted her again, "You home?"-Dylan. Not even the pesky little gray bubbles appeared to get his hopes up. *God, man, you are not getting close, you have officially crossed over into stalker territory,* he thought as he gazed at the dark house.

He reached into the back seat and pulled out a beer, popped the top and took a sip. He knew this was crazy and he was over the edge. He also knew he could lose not only a budding relationship with Autumn, but he could lose his job, yet, here he was, and here he was going to stay until he got some answers. He took another sip and then leaned back and closed his eyes. Even with his numbed state his cop senses were trying to tell him something.

The memory hit him like the splash of a salty ocean wave. His eyes flew open, but the mental image kept playing as vividly as an IMAX movie. Kate laughing and tossing him the keys, then the side of her neck exploding as her eyes grew wide and her lips transformed into a small O. Her eyes locked with his as she seemed to melt into the pavement. He found himself on the ground with her, but he had no memory of his movement to get there. As he cradled her in his arms and called her name over and over, her blood soaked through his clothing as her life slipped away.

The shot that took Kate was not a hit, nor was it in the line of duty; it was simply a chance stray bullet from across the street. Two punk kids fighting over a girl. *Stupid way to go. Completely random.* But then, no matter how much you plan; life is random.

Dylan gazed at the can of beer in his hand and said, "What are you doing?" He got out of his car and poured the contents into the gravel drive, then tossed the empty back into his car.

He approached the front door and knocked softly. Sadie went crazy on the other side of the door. "Sadie is mom home?" he asked through the door. *This is a mistake, McAlister,* he thought. *Big mistake. But what if something is wrong?*

What if his cop sense was driving him more than his romantic sense? He had not wanted to say it aloud, or even to think it, but the thought followed him around all evening like a mosquito buzzing and buzzing. He didn't know Autumn well, but well enough to think she wouldn't simply blow him off without a call or even a text.

Now that he was allowing the train of thought to flow, the reasons he should be worried continued to build. *What about all the strange incidents since Autumn arrived in Lake Phillips?* He took a step back and listened to Sadie bark unchecked on the other side of the door. What if they were connected? Individually they weren't that bad, but if they were all linked, the entire situation became ominous.

It had all started with the dog. Why was she on Autumn's dock with her mouth bound and covered in human blood? Was it really a dog fighting ring when they could not seem to locate Jan Miller? And the weird scene at Jan Miller's house. Then there was the box of stuff and the display of the contents on her bed. Maybe kids, or an admirer, but maybe something a lot more sinister. When they found her ex-husband stabbed to death, he assumed it had to do with his drug habit, but what if it had to do with Autumn instead? Each incident seemed to have a logical explanation, but when you thought about it, there was too much going on not to consider Autumn was in danger.

He gazed at the house and let his eyes trail up to the second floor as Sadie kept barking, but no lights came on. *Something isn't right, either she isn't at home or she is injured,* he thought. He shook his head and then remembered the bizarre crime scene at Jan Miller's house and the resemblance of her and Autumn in the photographs. The chill that traveled up his spine made him feel suddenly very sober and his fatigue disappeared.

Dylan shook the door handle, but it was locked, so he made his way around the back of the house and climbed the stairs to the deck. The deck door was also locked but the curtains were open. He could see Sadie whining on the other side of the picture window as her nose kept poking against the window. He took a step back and looked up at the second story balcony. *Maybe she forgot to lock it again*, he thought. He dragged a chair over and climbed up on the deck railing. He was surprised at how easy it was to reach the second story deck. One hard pull and he was up and over.

The curtain to the deck door was open, but the slider door was locked. He found himself looking directly into Autumn's bedroom, but it was dark and empty, and her bed was still neatly made. Sadie panted on the other side of the door, then jumped up on the glass with both front paws resting against the slider. Dylan could see where the dog had relieved herself on the hard wood floor by the door. As well trained an animal as she was, Dylan had no doubt that Autumn had not been home all day or evening. He looked at the dog and his heart twisted. It seemed that now not just Sadie's original owner was missing, so was her adoptive mom.

He climbed down from the balcony and circled the house as he checked all the doors and windows, but they were all locked. He went to the back of the house and climbed the stairs to the 1st floor deck. He didn't want to break the back door but the window over the kitchen sink was old and needed replacing anyway. He looked around and then smiled as he pulled the gun he carried at his ankle and used the butt to shatter and clear the glass before he climbed through. Most of the glass remained in the sink, but he swept up the rest of it so none of the animals would be injured before he fed them. He headed to the front door and shut off the alarm. Autumn gave him the code to put in her file when she had it installed. It was when he was still cop Dylan and not stalker, possible boyfriend, Dylan.

After he put food in the animal's dishes, he leaned against the counter and watched them eat. As they were wolfing down the food he turned and looked at the window. He was pretty sure he could find a board in the basement that would cover it until he could make the repairs. His eyes trailed from the now open window to a little guitar beer opener hanging by the window. It was brightly painted red and white and it reminded him of the night he listened to Autumn play and sing for the first time. Tears stung his eye and he turned from it and headed for the basement in search of a board. She was still alive. This could not be happening to him again. It just couldn't.

Chapter 19

Autumn thought as she heard a noise coming from the door to her cell. She kept her eyes closed and her body still as she tried to control her breathing. She was lying on the cot and realized she must have given herself up to sleep at some point. Her senses tingled, and she could almost feel the shift in air as the door opened, but she refused to show any sign of recognition.

I am asleep, go away. Maybe if she thought it hard enough he would believe it, because she really did not want to find out why the room was soundproofed. She could smell food and sensed a presence in the room, but she could not, would not open her eyes and look.

"I know you are awake, Michelle."

Her eyelids slid up and she adjusted her head until she had a full view of the door. The blue-eyed spidery man stood holding a tray and the door remained open behind him. *God, he is tall and skinny,* she thought. He had a sloppy smile and wore an expression that she would have read as affection if she didn't know he was like a snake who could strike at any moment.

Autumn pushed herself up to a seated position on the cot and glared at him. Her hands clutched at the side of the mattress where the sheet tucked into the iron frame as she prepared to spring forward if necessary, but the chain that weighed down on her ankle reminded her it was futile, hence the open door. It was an invitation and torture at the same time. Autumn hated to see dogs tethered on a stake in yards, now she knew how they felt: scared, angry, and ready to fight.

Spindly man smiled and said, "I knew it. You did that when we were little. Playing possum was your favorite game when you were in the *special room.*" She tilted her head to one side and thought, *What are you talking about?*

Something flickered in his eyes, a deep sadness that gave him a haunted look, but it only lasted a moment, then the strangely, almost manic happy face reappeared. If she chose an emoji to describe him at this moment it would be the big yellow smiley face. *Creepy,* she thought and shivered.

"I bet you are hungry," he said as he crossed the room in two strides and placed the tray on the bed beside her, then he backed up and leaned against the wall as he stared down at her. "Go ahead, eat. I'm sure you will love it. I made it exactly like you like it."

She glanced at the tray. A bowl of tomato soup and a cheese sandwich with no crust and a sprig of grapes on a blue china plate. A glass of milk and two chocolate chip cookies on a smaller matching plate completed the meal. She wanted to scream and throw it at him, but instead she took a breath, looked at him and said, "Who are you?"

A wide grin from him and then he winked and said, "You know who I am, Michelle. I know you love games almost as much as me, but I don't like this one."

Her mind started an extensive mental dialog as she fought to keep her face neutral. *Me playing games? You are the nutcase Mr. Psycho spider man; setting all this up and playing out some weird fantasy.* But she said, "No, I don't know who you are, and my name is Autumn, not Michelle." She glanced at the open door again and mentally kicked herself. He most likely got off on her feeling trapped and if she kept looking at that door she was playing into his fantasy.

He grimaced, then rolled his eyes and said, "Autumn is the name *they* gave you, but Michelle is your real name, Michelle O'Brien. Please don't tell me you don't remember any of this."

Her eyes narrowed, and she said, "You mean that was my name before I was adopted?"

"Precisely." He grinned and crossed his long thin arms as he leaned into the padded wall.

She had him. "I was abandoned at a Catholic orphanage, so there is nothing known about my earlier life. So, you see, you have the wrong woman." She felt a chill as she realized she shouldn't antagonize him if he held all the power.

"You should be able to figure this out quicker, Michelle. I know you don't have my IQ, but you were still smarter than anyone else I knew." He frowned and said, "Unless you don't want to remember me." He sighed and then said, "All, right; I'll play along. I know all about you because my mother, our mother, told me where she left you." A deeper frown and he said, "She actually used it as a threat repeatedly. She was such a fool sometimes. I understood from the beginning that you were the lucky one and I dreamed of her dropping me off to find a new family."

"*What?*" Autumn stood and waved her hands, "What are you talking about?"

"I am your brother, Michelle, your twin brother to be exact." He moved between her and the door and then said, "Superfecundation twins."

"*What?*" she asked again, but then sat heavily on the cot before she said it once again in a voice that dropped to a whisper, "What?"

"Oh, Michelle, come on, you sound like a dumb parrot. I know you understand what I'm saying. We may be superfecundation twins, but we still have some of the same DNA coursing through us and I have a genius level IQ."

"What the hell is 'super, uh, superfecundation twins?" She clasped her hands in her lap to keep from jumping off the cot and punching the crazy fool in the throat. *Where is he getting all this stuff? Is he a garden variety stalker, or is there some truth to what he is saying?*

"Superfecundation twins have the same mother but different fathers."

"You made that up," she said as she gazed at him.

He laughed, shook his head, and said, "You might think so, and it does sound rather barbaric, but it is a fact. We are rare. As rare as a blue dendrobium orchid, but it is a real thing just like the orchid." He leaned against the wall again and nodded toward the tray and said, "Please, eat."

Autumn frowned and looked at the tray. She was starving, but what if the food was drugged? *So, what if it is?* she thought. She was shackled to a bed and trapped in a soundproofed room. Maybe being drugged would help her cope with whatever was coming. She shrugged and picked up half of the sandwich and took a bite. It was delicious. Somehow that pissed her off even more than she was before. She gazed up at him and her eyes narrowed as she swallowed and said, "So, you are supposed to be my brother and 'our' mother gave me away but kept you? Why?"

A deep sigh from him. "That, dear Michelle, is the million-dollar question I have struggled with for my entire life." He squatted with his back still firmly planted against the wall. He was much more vulnerable in that position, but the strength she felt earlier in those thin arms convinced her she had to wait. She needed more than the element of surprise. It was crucial that she have some sort of weapon to equal the playing field. A glance at the tray. It was metal. It could work, but she wasn't sure how fast she could move with the chain on her leg, and she knew he could move lightning fast. She glanced back up when he continued with, "Admittedly, I never gave her any fight, at least not as a child, and you were always standing up to her. But, I suspect the real reason was she didn't like women, or girls, only men, and would get jealous of any female in the vicinity, and even though you were just a little girl, the men would look at you." He shrugged and said, "Who knows why she did any of the things

158

she did. She also did a lot of drugs, so she could have simply gotten really stoned and forgot you somewhere."

Autumn was stunned into silence, but she felt the need to keep him talking. Maybe he would let something slip that could help her escape. "Okay, so, who is our mother and father, uh fathers?" She took another bite, then gulped some water from the bottle on the table beside the bed. She didn't even like milk. She stared at him and thought, *I wonder why he didn't know that if he claims to know me so well?*

"Was. *Was*, dear sister. Our mother is departed from this realm." He rose to his full height. An image of a large praying mantis skittered through her thoughts. "You may not remember, and admittedly it was a long time ago, but our mother entertained a lot of men back then, and she wasn't very picky if they had adequate funds. She told me my father was a college student who got too eager for her to use protection, and your father was actually her real boyfriend who refused to obey the same rules as her many Johns."

Autumn stopped eating and looked at him. "Our mother was a hooker and she actually told you that?"

"Hooker, prostitute, lady of the evening, although I wouldn't use lady in any form to describe our mother; she was whatever euphemism you wish to use, but yes, she traded sex for money, and yes, she enjoyed telling me lots of things about her men, and the story of our fathers. She said she didn't know which of them was our daddy, but I found out, with a little research, that they both were; one for each of us."

Autumn had a flash of the dream when she was in the closet with the blue-eyed boy and the hairy man. "The closet..." she mumbled.

"You are remembering, now, aren't you?" He clapped his hands and she jumped as the sound reverberated in the small room.

"I dreamt of it after the teddy bear came." She looked up at him, "That was you, wasn't it?"

"Oh, yes. You loved that bear so much that I saved him for you all these years." He bowed and said, "You're welcome."

"I dreamed about this chain on my leg, too," she said as she rattled the chain with her leg.

"Oh, I'm sorry about that, but it has to stay for a while." Autumn didn't think he looked the least bit sorry as he moved toward the door, but then he turned back to her and said, "Yes, I did learn that little trick from mom. She began to chain us to our bed in what she called *the special room* after the closet incident with that man. It was fashioned much like this room, but it was just a big closet. She didn't want to upset her 'clients' was the way she put it. She was such a sweetheart that way." He glanced at the walls and said, "She didn't use this soundproofing material, she used old mattresses to pad the walls, so her friends couldn't hear us. It was disgusting. I couldn't do that when I created my holding rooms, so I used only the best materials and tried to make it homier."

Autumn looked at the padding, and for an instant it faded and soiled old mattresses appeared. She shook her head to clear the vision and then looked back at her captor. She didn't want to admit the thought, or possible memory, so she said, "What did she look like?"

His eyes went dead, and he said, "Just look in the mirror. Unfortunately, you look just like her, but then again, she was beautiful on the outside."

He started moving through the door, but Autumn said, "Wait, I have more questions." She hated the whine she heard in her voice but couldn't seem to help it. As much as this man frightened her, the idea of more hours being shut in this cubicle alone was worse.

No smile as he turned toward her, and the blue eyes were flat as he said, "I have to go now. I have some things to do and you must be tired. Finish your food and rest, I'll be back later."

"Wait, what do I call you?"

"Oh, Michelle, that hurts. You don't remember my name? It's Rowen, Rowen O'Brian." The door shut, and he was gone.

Autumn didn't know if she should believe a single word he just said. The man was certifiable. However, it explained the dreams she was having. *Memories instead of dreams?* It could be. And what was with those mattresses she saw? She was awake when she got that vision. Did she really have some sort of memory block and the block was fading? Or was it all simply the power of suggestion?

She picked up one of the cookies and began to chew as she tried to remember more, but then she mumbled, "Bat shit crazy," and went back to thinking about how she could get free. She dropped the cookie on the plate as she remembered her resemblance to Jan Miller. The looney said Autumn looked just like 'their' mother, so perhaps he was simply choosing victims who resembled mommy dearest. But, what about the dreams, she thought. She shook her head and said, 'Enough." The rest of it didn't matter. Getting free was where her mind needed to be.

***

Dylan knocked on Pat and Terri's door. He glanced down at Sadie and said, "It's okay, girl. We are going to find her." She looked up at him and whined. He knew how she felt, even as he said the words he felt no conviction in them.

By the time he cleaned up Sadie's accidents, fed her and the cats, and put a board over the window he broke, the dawn was breaking. He then sat in the kitchen and sipped coffee from Autumn's stash of caffeine until he felt it was a decent enough time to knock on her neighbor's door.

Although he searched Autumn's house from top to bottom, nothing seemed out of place other than a full cup of coffee abandoned on the kitchen counter. At least there was nothing like what they found at Jan Miller's house. No signs of a struggle and no blood. Her purse was there, but her keys and her cell phone were gone. He was relieved not to find evidence of a crime, but still anxious. Autumn did not strike him as the type of person who would abandon her animals without something dire happening. He didn't feel like he could report it to the station. They would look at him with pity, or worse, laugh in his face. Without any evidence of it being anything more than an overnight at someone's house, he only had his gut to go on.

Dylan hoped Autumn would understand about the window and his interference at the house, and his multiple text and phone messages. If she was simply out on an overnight date, she was going to kill him, but if she really was missing, well, he didn't want to think about that right now.

"Hi, Dylan," Terri said as she opened the door. She was dressed in a paint splattered blue work shirt over old jeans and equally splattered tennis shoes. She was petit, and, in that outfit, she could have passed for a teenager from behind. A glance at Sadie and she continued with, "Everything all right?" A look of concern on her face as she gazed into Dylan's eyes. He knew he must look terrible after two nights without sleep.

"I hope so, but I'm not sure." He nodded toward Autumn's house and said, "Uh, I couldn't reach Autumn last night, so I stopped by and Sadie sounded as if she was in distress, so I, uh, went in, and it looked like Autumn has not been home in some time. Sadie had a few accidents and the cats were hungry, so I fed them all and cleaned up the mess. I waited to see if Autumn came home, but I must have fallen asleep on the couch." A little white lie, but he simply couldn't tell this woman about the window and no sleep. He wanted her to take him seriously, not feel like she needed to have him committed.

"Oh, my, that doesn't sound like Autumn." She ran a paint covered hand through her blonde locks and left a smear of blue on her bangs.

"Uh, you got a little paint there," he said as he pointed at her hair.

She rolled her eyes up toward her bangs and said, "Oh, good grief, I'm always forgetting when I paint." She gazed at her hands and said, "Come in Dylan, and bring Sadie. I'm going to go wash this off." She stood back, and he entered the Cape Cod style cottage. He stayed in the entry as she started up the stairs toward the second story. "Make yourself comfortable in the den. I won't be long." She continued up the stairs, then paused and turned as she said, "Close the sliders to the deck so Sadie won't get paint on herself as well." Then laughed and took the stairs two at a time.

As Dylan made his way through the house he admired the style of the cottage. He visited them several times for social events and never failed to feel at ease in the house. When he reached the den, he moved to the slider and shut the door. He stood for a moment as he gazed through the glass at the deck. Terri had moved the deck furniture and plants to one side and had almost finished with a fresh paint job on the deck. The blue hue sparkled in the morning sun. He heard footsteps and turned to see Terri coming. She had changed and had wet hair and paint free hands. Pat followed behind her and they both joined them in the den.

"How can we help?" Pat said as Terri got on her knees and petted Sadie. The dog rolled on her back and gazed up at her as she wiggled her approval. Terri laughed and scratched Sadie's chest and tummy. Their dog, a cute little mass of white fur, came bolting into the room and joined in as she started the wrestling session with the much larger dog.

Dylan smiled at the dogs who seemed perfectly at ease with each other. He said, "I have to get to work, but if you could take care of Sadie and keep an eye out for Autumn I would really appreciate it.

"Sure, no problem," Pat said. She laughed as she watched the dogs and added, "Looks like Daisy is ready for a playdate."

"Please let us know if you hear from her first," Terri added. "We are worried. Autumn struck us as a responsible person and we don't believe she would leave her animals like that."

"I agree. I am going to make some calls as soon as I get to the station and I will let you know if I find out anything."

As he drove toward home for a quick check on Ollie before he headed to work, his stomach churned as he remembered the scene at Jan Miller's house, and worse, the motel room covered in blood with Autumn's ex tied to a chair. "Please don't let this be connected," he mumbled as he stepped on the accelerator.

Chapter 20

Dylan sat at his desk and searched through his notes. Where was it? He dug through a stack of paperwork and frowned as he tried to remember the name of Richard's band. *Was it The Saints, no, that's not it, The Angels, The Devils…Purgatory! That's it!* As he remembered the name he found the paper that had their information and picked up the phone to call them.

"Dylan," Lucy said to him, "Madge and her kid want to see you and that warrant just came through."

He glanced up as he held the phone to his ear and said, "Okay, be right there."

"Sure, take your time--- I've just been babysitting them all morning, and the poor woman has barely left the station since he was arrested," she grumbled and turned her back to him.

He started to say something, but a male voice croaked on the other end of the phone and pulled his attention back to his call. He immediately forgot about Lucy. "Hello?" the gravelly voice said, then added, "What time is it?"

Dylan glanced at his watch and said, "11AM. This is Dylan McAlister with the Lake Phillips Police Department, we met at the tribute to Richard Scott."

"11AM? Man, what the hell?"

Dylan grimaced and sat back in his chair as he said, "Yes, as I was saying, this is Dylan McAlister with the police and I have some questions for you. Have you seen Autumn Brennan recently?"

"*What?* No, man. Not since we rocked it for her old man. Why?"

"You're sure? You didn't see her last night?" he asked as he sat forward and gripped the phone.

"No, of course not, unless she is in Nashville. We got home last night, or I should say we drove in a few hours ago."

"Oh, okay," Dylan said as his shoulders slumped.

"Hey, wait, is something wrong? Is she okay?"

"I'm not sure, that's why I'm calling, I, uh, we are trying to locate her."

"Oh, man, okay, listen, tell her to call me, okay? She's good people, so was Richard, but he had some, uh, issues. Anyway, tell her to let me know, okay?"

"All right, sure, I'll tell her to notify you as soon as I, uh, we locate her." Dylan disconnected and closed his eyes a moment as he thought, *Damn, damn, damn.*

"Dylan?" He glanced up and Officer Wilson was standing in front of him.

"What is it, Judy?"

"You okay? You look like crap," she said.

"Thanks, I'm fine. Nothing a little sleep wouldn't cure---What do you want?"

"That momma bear, Madge Brody refuses to talk to me, but she is demanding you get in there," she said, then snorted a low, "Bitch."

"Right, yeah, be right there," he said, then stood and headed for the men's room. He needed to get away from Wilson and splash water on his face. As he wiped the moisture away he gazed into the mirror and had to admit, at least to himself, that Judy Wilson was correct, he did look like crap, and it was only a little to do with not getting enough sleep.

Dylan left the men's room and almost collided with Judy Wilson. *Was she lurking out here the whole time?* he wondered.

"Are you going to talk to them or not?" She crossed her arms over her chest and stared at him as she waited for an answer. "They are getting pretty vocal about seeing you."

He looked at her and his vision blurred. Her image seemed to waver as her voice sounded as if it were coming from an echo chamber. He broke out in a cold sweat and realized he was about to faint. He leaned against the wall and swallowed hard to keep from puking in the middle of the Lake Phillips PD, then said, "Yes, but, tell her I have to go out on a call. Uh, tell her it has to do with her boy and it's important to their case." Another lie, but at this point who was counting?

Dylan needed to get home, eat, shower, and maybe sleep a few minutes before he could make even a half way intelligent conversation with them. Either that, or he was going to embarrass himself even more than he already had.

Wilson gazed at him and her eyebrows rose, then her eyes squeezed into a squint and she said, "Need backup?"

"What?" he said, then smiled and added, "No, just cover for me, okay? I'll be back soon." He pushed past her and kept going past Lucy's desk without another word. He could see the older woman's disapproving scowl out of his peripheral vision, but he didn't break his stride. Once in his car he drove straight to his cabin, fed and walked Ollie, showered and shaved, wolfed down the hamburger he had bought on the way home, then sat in his recliner.

He thought of Autumn and all the things that happened to her since she moved to the lake. He tried to think about the burglaries but couldn't focus on them. Autumn kept swirling through his sleep deprived brain. "Where are you?" he mumbled, then he closed his burning eyes and thought, *I'll just rest my eyes for a minute, then I will get back to the station,* before he slipped into a dark, velvety oblivion.

***

Autumn jumped and turned as the cell door opened. She was standing in front of her cot and staring up at the camera when she heard it swing outward. With the way the door was hung, there would be no hiding behind it to surprise her captor with her leg chain around his neck or a bash over the head if she found a weapon.

She spent the afternoon examining every corner of the room. She even experimented with pulling some of the soundproofing away from the wall as she glared up at the camera, but there was nothing under the padding but drywall and studs. There was no hope of escape from the padded cubicle. *At least not so far.* She could not even find something she could use as a weapon after he had taken the metal tray with him.

"You didn't rest," he said.

It wasn't issued as a question, but as a statement. She assumed he was watching her through that stupid camera mounted above the door. That must be his thing, *watching.* Just like he was watching her with the telescope from across the lake. "I wasn't tired," she said. She had to bite back the first retort that the flame of anger pushed into her mouth.

Anger wasn't going to work here, no matter how satisfying it would feel to express it. She had to be very careful with this man. He may be looney tunes, but he was smart as hell and held all the power. She was aware that provoking him might result in producing a side of the man she did not want to see.

Spindly man, or Rowen, or her brother if he was telling the truth, was holding a pile of clothing that he handed to her as he said, "Please, dress in these and we can have a nice family dinner."

Autumn gazed at the clothes, then up at him. "Okay, but you will need to leave and not watch me on your little eye above the door."

He laughed and said, "Oh, Michelle, that is just gross. Even if you weren't my sister, which you are, I would have no interest in your female form. My physical interests are, uh, shall we say firmly rooted in another direction." He grinned but turned around and waited for her to change. "I will respect your modesty. I find it's incredibly rare with your gender."

"Okay, but you need to take this off if you want me to change," she said then shook her ankle and the chain rattled.

He turned back around toward her and said, "Of course, but no peeking." He bent over her ankle with his back to her. She tried to see around him but couldn't make out the combination letters as he keyed them into the lock. She only glimpsed the first one, "M." She could hear the tumbles as he turned to the correct letters and she noted the time it took for each turn, but it would still take an infinite number of tries to get the combo correct. Her shoulders slumped; it would be an impossible task.

When she was free she bent and rubbed her ankle. It was red and sore where the heavy chain rested. Autumn picked up the clothes he gave her and examined them. They were of another era, probably from the 70's from the pattern and color, and they had a slight scent of cedar and some sort of incense that tickled her nose. The last thing she wanted to do was put them on, but she had to play along until she could gain some sort of leverage.

Autumn shed her outer wear and pulled on the pants and top and felt as if she had slipped back into a time warp when disco was supreme. Bell bottom hip hugger jeans with big belt loops, a snug tie-dyed T-shirt and wedge cork sandals with elaborate straps. *No belt for the jeans.* He was certainly keeping the theme of not giving her anything to work with as a weapon. She shivered and wondered if this was some of her biological mother's clothing. She felt bile rising from her stomach but swallowed hard and managed to contain it. The nausea stemmed both from the thought of wearing a dead woman's clothing and that she had thought of her as her mother. "All right, I'm ready," she said when she was dressed.

He turned around and applauded. "Oh my god, you look fantastic," he said, then he produced a brush and began to tame her red hair into two braids. When he finished he pocketed the brush and tucked a daisy into one of the braids. He grinned and said, "Perfect!" He stepped back and said, "Wait," and then stepped out of the door a moment and returned holding a white instamatic camera. He snapped a picture of her as a round flash popped on the top of it and a faint burning smell hung in the room. A photo shot out of the front with a whirring noise, then he grabbed it and waved it in the air before examining the image with a grin. "Excellent," he said as he held it up for her to see.

The image was grainy, and Autumn didn't recognize herself in the hippie gear. She shivered as she viewed it and thought it must make her look even more like *their* mother. She swallowed hard again. "Okay," was all she could manage to say.

Rowen gripped her arm and led her out of the padded room and they started down a long dark hallway. The floor consisted of old brown tiles and the walls were walnut wood paneling. It was styled in what seemed to be his preferred era, the 1970's. The man was stuck in another time.

Autumn's sandals made a clop, clop sound as they walked through the empty hallway. She glanced at the elaborate crisscrossed ties of the sandals that ran up her ankles and realized she would not be able to simply kick them off if she got a chance to run. *Smart thinking on his part, or just dumb luck?* It didn't matter; either way was going to impede her escape if the opportunity came up.

As they walked through the hallway, Autumn noticed several doors with the same kind of dead bolt lock that was on the outside of the door instead of on the inside, but she also noticed the only one with the lock engaged was the one next to her room. She heard nothing coming from the space, but the soundproofing would have taken care of that. He did say 'rooms' when describing how he created her cell. Autumn couldn't help but wonder if it was Jan Miller inside the other locked room. *Maybe she was still alive.*

Once they left the hallway Autumn blinked and gazed around. They were in the same massive basement area where she entered the house. All the curtains were still drawn, but there were several lamps giving off some soft lighting in the main section of the room. She wasn't sure what time it was, but she suspected it was dark outside.

As they passed a table Autumn noticed a large plastic bird perched on a stand. It had electronic equipment attached to it and what looked like a remote control beside it. Her mouth fell open as she thought, *I've seen that thing hovering around my house. Damn, what I thought was a bird was a damn drone.* She pressed her lips together but kept quiet. *No use giving him the pleasure of my reaction, but that's how he was watching me so closely.*

Rowen led her across the room to a dining table that was set with a white lacy tablecloth and two elaborate place settings. In the center of the table two red taper candles were the only lighting for this side of the room. Each plate was loaded with delicious smelling food and there were two crystal wine glasses brimming with a deep red wine.

He pulled her chair out and waited until she was seated before he sat in the chair to her left. To the right was the wall covered with the pictures that drew her into the room the day before. *Had it only been one day?* she thought.

Autumn stared at the wall. She tried not to, but it was impossible. At the center of the display was her 8 x 10 professional shot, but now that she was closer, she could see numerous photos of herself going about her daily activities. *Thanks to the drone.* She felt her face grow hot and knew she was flushed as she continued to stare at the collection.

There were pictures from her childhood, some taken in Nashville, her moving day here in Lake Phillips, ones of her and Richard, even a few shots of her through the window of her lake house. He must have a high-powered photo lens on that damn drone. The man was truly a voyeur. *How long has he been watching me without my knowledge and where did he get my childhood photographs?*

She could feel him staring at her as her eyes followed the display from top to bottom, but as hard as she tried, she couldn't stop herself from her intensive perusal. She felt like she did when she drove past a bad accident on the highway and didn't want to look, but her eyes betrayed her.

Once she reached the bottom photos she gasped and heard him chuckle. Her head slowly turned toward him, and she asked, "Is that Jan Miller? Did you kill her and those other women?"

He nodded and giggled, then said, "I chose Jan especially because I knew you would love that dog. You always loved dogs, and Jan looked so much like you, well, I just knew the creature would take to you. And it was a golden retriever, just like the one your adoptive parents gave you." He frowned and added, "She was such a disappointment, though, not much fun at all, and that disgusting dog—I had to fashion a muzzle out of duct tape because even sedated, she kept trying to bite me." He stood and moved over to the wall and tacked the photo he just took of Autumn in the bottom section.

Autumn felt the familiar heat rising in her face and tried clinching her fists under the table and counting in her head. *One; don't react, two; be cool, three; don't react...*

He grinned at her and sat back down. She felt as if he could read her thoughts, when he said, "I know, I know. You hate any kind of cruelty to all fur things, but Michelle, this dog was being a real bitch. She sure quieted down once I took her mom out of her miserable life. The woman wasn't strong like the rest of you and so it was no fun to play the game with her."

"Game?"

He gazed at the wall and tented his hands in a prayer like stance under his chin. His light blue eyes sparked in the candle light and a look of bliss played across his features. "The game is everything and eventually they decide playing it is fun, but if they start obeying right away it ruins it. I like them to welcome the knife, but it should take a little while, you know? Jan was much too quick." He looked back at her and said, "But you got the dog, so it was worthwhile. Hey, if you are enjoying these highlights, I should really share my movies with you."

Autumn became a statue. A cold piece of marble. She was frozen and couldn't move. She mumbled through dry, parched lips, "Why? Why are you doing this? I thought you said you didn't like women in that way..." She hadn't intended to vocalize her judgement, it simply wouldn't stay inside. Her voice trailed off as she noticed his expression and she silenced the words that wanted to explode from her and gripped her hands together to keep from striking him.

He frowned as he looked at her and said, "Of, course I don't think of them like that. Don't be disgusting. *Sex* doesn't have anything to do with it. I *romance* them. I tell them what they long to hear. They love that. It's what momma really wanted. It has nothing to do with sex." He gazed at her and said, "I thought you would be flattered I noticed how much you enjoyed the dog from your childhood." His lip protruded in a pout and he looked back at the pictures on the wall and said, "I give them the attention and romance they crave, but once I bring them home, I give them what they all really need, -- a little discipline."

Autumn gripped the edges of the table and said, "But you kill them, why?"

He shrugged and grinned, "Honestly, I don't know why, but it makes me happy, so I don't look too closely at the *why*. I could give you all kinds of psychobabble about it, believe me, I have done the research. I hated our mother, I hate all women, they pissed me off, yadda, yadda. But what it really comes down to is this; I make them happy then they make me happy. Thus, the game." He sighed and gazed at Autumn and continued with, "It's a symbiotic relationship. They are taken out of their lonely miserable lives and enjoy a cloud of romantic haze, then I take what I need for a little while, and then dispatch them quickly with the knife. I don't need to over think it. I save my considerable brain power to figure out how to do it, not why. Who cares why." He took a sip of wine and gazed back at the photo gallery as he said, "Just a hobby. That's all. A little game to amuse."

Autumn searched her mind to come up with a response that didn't drip with the disgust she felt, or at least more questions that wouldn't sound judgmental. She needed to make him feel like she was a companion, a sister and a confidant, not paint herself like a victim, or reveal the revulsion and horror she was feeling. "Why, these women? I understand the obvious, that they look like me, so they must look like, uh, our mother, but Jan Miller was independent and a successful woman. She was nothing like the picture you paint of our mother being a prostitute," she said.

"Don't believe it; she was weak when it really came down to it, not independent at all, and it is as you said, they were chosen for the obvious reason that they look like our mother." A smile as he gazed toward the hallway to her cell. He turned back to her and made eye contact as he said, "I started with a few prostitutes, but like I said, it was no fun. First, they didn't respond well to romance and they only wanted money. Second, it was too easy. Wave a few bucks and they will follow you anywhere, say anything, dress any way you want." He grimaced and said, "Where's the fun in that? So, I stumbled on a woman who looked exactly like mom but was almost unreachable. I took a tremendous chance, because she was a consultant for my business. She was successful, worked all the time, and had no interest in dating. Now, she was what I considered a challenge, and it was *delicious*." He leaned back and stroked his chin as he said, "Especially when I got her to dress and act like our mother."

"Was? I assume that means she is dead?" Autumn asked.

He looked toward the door to the patio. The curtain was pulled tight, so he couldn't see out, but he stared at it as he said in a faraway, dreamy voice, "Yes, but I keep them with me in their pictures, my little movies, and in other ways. It's fun. They are always here, but no one knows. Here but not here." He looked back at her and then let his eyes travel back to the montage of photos.

Autumn shook her head and tried to gather her thoughts. She didn't want to show disgust, but it was difficult not to have it distort her facial expression. She practiced relaxing her face from her eyes down through her mouth as she stared at him. This man, for god's sake, *possibly her brother, her twin brother*, was completely, totally insane, and she needed to keep from setting him off. *How can I be related to this horror show,* ran through her thoughts, but she said, "How long have you been here? I mean, at this house on Lake Phillips. I only just got here, how did you set this place up so fast?" she asked. Autumn was shocked at how calm her voice sounded. She reached for the wine glass, but her trembling hand was certain to give her away, so she gripped her hands together in her lap instead.

He laughed and said, "Genius, dear sister; it was pure genius!" He leaned back and said, "I set this in motion long before you even thought about buying a house here. It is perfect for my needs because of the isolation. So, after I was firmly established, I started sending you little advertising hints about getting away and starting fresh. And when I felt like you were ready, I was the one who sent you the real estate emails with the pictures of your little rundown palace located on peaceful Lake Phillips. I knew it would get your creative juices flowing. Then I made sure the sale went smoothly for you."

Autumn wanted to punch him in his face, but instead she said, "That was you? You did all that? But, everyone said this house you are living in is vacant---How did you manage that?"

"Oh, Michelle, don't be so naive. Money gets you whatever you want. I insisted that joke of a real estate agent list this house as vacant. I told her it was for my privacy, but I've owned it and operated out of here for a very long time. Then it was simply a matter of bringing you here and that was so much easier than I expected. Honey, you were ripe. The only time I got a little worried was when that ass wipe followed you here, but that was an easy remedy. Actually, I rather enjoyed that a lot."

Autumn sucked in a breath and said, "*Richard?*"

He nodded and said, "You're welcome."

Certifiable, Autumn thought. She gazed at her cutlery and noticed there was no knife. *He said he has a high IQ, but he is also arrogant and a narcissist, so maybe, just maybe,* she thought. She could use his arrogance and vanity to keep herself from ending up as just another photo on the bottom of that wall. *Maybe...*

Chapter 21

As Dylan entered the room Madge Brody asked, "When are we getting out of here? We have been waiting all day." Her face was flushed, and she sat on the edge of her chair as she leaned across the desk.

"We are working on it Madge," Dylan said as he sat behind the desk. "Your boy is still under arrest, but we are going to get him released in your custody as soon as we can confirm his information."

"Why hasn't that already been done?"

"Something else that was critical came up and caused a delay, but Josh is still a priority, and we have the warrant to go into the house he told us about." He turned to the boy and said, "Now Josh, you aren't sending us on a wild goose chase, are you? You stated you and Timmy saw something suspicious; some photographs that looked like someone was killed? It will not go well for you if you are lying, because you don't want to take valuable time away from other important ongoing investigations."

Dylan reddened as he thought about the time he wasted napping, but he honestly didn't think he could be functioning right now without it. When he woke up in his chair and looked at his watch, he ran from the house and drove here breaking all the speed limits. He understood her frustration with the time lapse. They must be ready to climb the walls.

Autumn was still foremost on his mind, but he needed to get this taken care of. He exhausted every avenue he could think of in looking for her, but still, he didn't want to be wasting time at an empty house because something spooked a couple of kids when he could be searching for Autumn. Dylan checked with the hospital and other departments in the county, but so far nothing. He called Pat & Terri on the way to the station, but they didn't notice anything unusual in the neighborhood and hadn't heard from her, either.

Autumn had vanished. *Just like Jan Miller*, he thought, but then he pushed the idea away. He needed to concentrate on this case before it got away from him. It was getting late and he should have already served the warrant on the house. He had a nagging feeling that somehow all this was connected but couldn't imagine how. Too many strange occurrences in such a small district could not be ignored.

The boy's eyes widened with Dylan's threat and he looked at his mother. She nodded at him and turned to Dylan and said, "We don't believe we are wasting your time. The pictures the boys saw might have been faked, but they really scared them. The house Josh told you about is listed as a vacant house that is available and on the market. Josh went in thinking it was empty, but the truth is, the man who bought it has been living there for a while. He is a wealthy man with a big computer company in DC. He told me that he must protect his privacy for business concerns, but I suspected at the time that it was because he is a bit of a recluse. Josh didn't know about any of this. I was paid to keep it quiet, but I think that it was a little suspicious and should have sent up a red flag for me." Her head dropped as she continued with, "So, if anyone has gotten hurt it's my fault not Josh's. The money was too attractive for me to question the reason why he wanted so much secrecy."

Josh patted his mother's arm and said, "No, this is on me, mom." He turned to Dylan and said, "No sir, I'm not making any of this up; both Timmy and I really saw those pictures. I'm not promising they're still there, or that they are real, but they were spooky. The whole top area of the photo wall was covered with pictures of some red headed lady, not nasty pictures, just regular photos, and the ones at the bottom were different and scary. Timmy thought it looked like one lady in the strange pictures was dead, but I told him it was photoshopped." The boy took a breath and added, "There was a drone, too. It could be used to take secret pictures without the ladies knowing about it, oh, and a telescope. Some guys are into that kind of stuff. You should be able to at least bust him for illegal internet stuff. No telling what he posted from his drone pictures." A glance at his mother, then he continued with, "I don't personally know about that kind of *shi*, uh stuff, but other guys told me about seeing porn like that on the dark web. I don't know if the lady in the grainy picture is dead or if it's fake, but it certainly was weird and worth checking out."

Dylan stared at the boy with a frozen expression as his heart began beating very fast. Everything the boy said after 'red headed lady' was hard to hear over the thump, thump of his heartbeat sounding in his ears. Dylan pulled out his phone and scrolled through his pictures until he found the one he snapped of Autumn at dinner. She was laughing at him and the image pulled at his heart, but he showed it to Josh and asked, "Did the redhead look like this lady?"

Josh squinted at the picture and said, "The more modern pictures were that lady, the one's that she was doing regular stuff in, but, I don't think that was her in the bottom bondage type pictures. Those ladies looked a little different, but it could just be the photos because it was hard to see details and they looked old timey."

Dylan got up so abruptly that his chair fell backwards as he rushed from the room. He grabbed a file off his desk and sprinted back into the room and slapped it in front of the boy. He flipped the file open to the photo of Jan Miller and asked Josh, "What about this woman?"

"Hey, that's her---the one Timmy thought was dead." He paled and looked up at Dylan and added, "This is real, isn't it? Oh, man."

Dylan nodded a tight nod and said, "Yes, it is, and the other woman, the one you said there were a lot of pictures of, well, she is missing."

"Oh, my God," Madge said as her face paled.

Dylan looked at her and said, "You said it was a single man living in the house? Do you know him? You can give us all his information?"

"Oh, yes, yes---" she said.

Dylan nodded and left the room. In the hallway he saw Judy Wilson and he shouted, "Wilson, you're with me. We are serving this warrant."

***

Rowen stood and said, "It's been lovely, Michelle, just lovely being with you again, but it's time for you to go back to your room. I have some work I need to do now." He glanced at the wall of pictures, then turned and gazed at a laptop on a desk nearby before he looked back at her and smiled. She was being dismissed.

Autumn searched the dining table, but there was nothing left to eat or drink. She lingered as much as she dared over the meal and desert. The wine bottle was empty, although she had managed to let him consume most of the bottle, and both plates had nothing left but a few crumbs and a slash of chocolate where cake once resided.

Her smile felt stiff as she said, "Okay, but don't you want to visit a while longer? I didn't know I had any family and I would really like to hear more about our mother and what you have been doing all these years." She felt her voice quiver as she spoke, so she tried to cover it by clearing her throat. He was intelligent and not easily fooled, so she needed to be careful, but his ego was also huge, so she was hoping he would overlook her ploy to keep the chain off her ankle and buy a little more time out of that horrible room.

Rowen sat down and stared at her. She cringed inwardly and held her breath as his eyes narrowed, but then he said, "Our mother was cruel, ego centric, and without class, so I don't enjoy thinking or talking about her. I know it's natural for you to be curious, but don't be; there is nothing there for you. She may have given birth to us, but she was never motherly. You were the lucky one, but then, you always were. Being abandoned was the best thing that could have

180

happened to you."

She reached out a hand and touched his lightly before she pulled it back and said, "I'm sorry you had to deal with that. I don't remember much about it, at least not yet, but it seems to be coming back to me in bits and pieces." A sigh, then she continued with, "From what I dreamt, you must have had it rough." She realized that this time her words weren't just a ploy for time, she meant what she said. He went through hell as a child, but that still didn't give him carte blanche to inflict so much cruelty on innocent women.

He gazed at the picture display again and said in a low voice that was almost a whisper, "I got away from her as soon as I was able to make any kind of life on my own. I was about fifteen when I ran away. I lived on the streets at first and did have to provide services for a few older men when I was making my way, so I did a little of following in dear old mom's footsteps. But I didn't stay there, and it was my intellect that got me off the streets and provided scholarships that got me my degrees and wealth." A shadow moved over his features and his eyes went flat. He stood and picked up his flatware and stacked it onto his plate then looked at her and said, "As soon as I landed my first big job she showed up on my doorstep. Literally, there she stood with an old suitcase pleading for me to take her in. I'm not sure how she found me, or if she knew where I was all along, but she didn't bother with me until I had some money rolling in. Her looks were pretty much gone by then, and she was into drugs and booze big time, but I still let her stay. I hated her with all my being but I'm not a monster. She was our mother after all." He shrugged and gazed at Autumn and said, "You look so much like her. The earlier version before her looks went."

Autumn felt a chill and realized she did think of him as a monster, but it was most likely his mother that made him into one. *Our mother if what he is telling me is true,* she thought, then asked, "Do you have any pictures of her?"

A sad smile that turned into an unreadable expression as he said, "A few, but none to share."

"Uh, okay. Can I ask what happened to her? You said she is dead?"

He turned away a moment, and then turned back and looked at Autumn. The smile he wore made her scoot back in her chair as her stomach tightened. He said in a soft, dreamy voice, "She died in her sleep one night after ingesting a few too many of her favorite pills. A much better ending than she deserved. She should have suffered more; I should have made her suffer more." Another sigh, then he said, "I had her cremated and she is still in my DC penthouse." He walked around to the back of Autumn's chair and pulled it away from the table as he said, "Now I really need to get to work. We will have plenty of time to talk soon."

He walked around and stood in front of Autumn as he gestured with one hand in the direction of her room, then dropped both hands to his sides. She noticed his hands were clinched into fists. *Don't push him too far*, she thought, so she got up and said, "Can I help you with the dishes? You prepared such a nice meal, so I would love to do my part."

He glared at her, then sighed and said, "Michelle, I know you are stalling because you don't want to go back to your room. You did the same thing with mother when you didn't want to go to bed, but it didn't work with her and it won't work with me." He took a small step toward her.

She stood her ground, grinned and said, "You're right, and you do seem to know me, but must I go back to that room and wear the chain? You can trust me, brother."

He cocked his head to one side and said, "Maybe we will get there someday, maybe we won't, but that day is not today. Please don't make me angry. I do not want to get angry with you and I have some important work to do."

She held up her hands and said, "Okay, sorry, Rowen." She pushed her chair up to the table, but as he turned and again gestured for her to lead the way, she lunged for the empty wine bottle sitting on the dining room table.

Autumn played a lot of baseball when she was in high school and was the best batter on her senior year team, so she used that same motion, along with all the momentum the lunge granted her, and hit him hard on the side of his head. It felt like the same amount of force as when she hit a homerun against Jamie Reese in the end of season game, and it gave her the same feeling of elation.

As the bottle connected with the side of Rowen's head it made a loud *thunk* sound and he went down onto one knee. Since the bottle did not break on the initial contact, she raised it again as high as her arms would reach, and then brought it down even harder on the same side of his head. This time the bottle shattered on impact and he went all the way to the floor. She pushed him with the toe of her sandal, but he didn't move, so she dropped the neck of the bottle and sat back down in her chair and began jerking at the laces of the sandals.

Autumn struggled with the complex laces, then said, "Crap," and grabbed the jagged wine bottle neck and cut them off before she was able to yank the platforms from her feet. One more check on the unconscious Rowen, then she ran.

She sprinted around the table to avoid the glass shards of the shattered wine bottle and headed to the back door. Without a glance back at the dining table she grabbed the door knob and pulled, but it was locked, so she flipped the dead bolt, jerked the door open, and ran out onto the back patio.

She paused and bent at the waist and sucked in several deep breaths. It was night and chilly, but the cool air in her lungs felt wonderful. She stood and gazed across the yard toward the water and could just make out the dark shape of her kayak against the white sand. A glance over her shoulder toward the side of the house leading to the road tempted her to keep running, but the water was her fastest escape route, besides, if Rowen woke up, he would surely catch her on the road with those long spindly legs of his.

She prepared to sprint forward, but then she hesitated. Autumn looked back at the house and thought about the locked door in that darkened hallway next to hers.

She should leave and send back help. She needed to get to a phone and it wasn't worth searching for her cell; Rowen probably destroyed it. She turned toward the lake and took a deep breath. Her shoulders slumped, and she shook her head.

What if there was another chained woman in that room? Rowen might wake up angry and decided to get rid of any loose ends, or even worse, decide to take his anger at Autumn's escape out on the hapless woman. Autumn started to run toward the lake, then swiveled, ran in place, groaned and said, "Damn!"

Chapter 22

Dylan left the village and began racing around the lake as he drove double the 25mph posted speed limit. The warrant was in his pocket and he had Judy Wilson call Lucy as soon as they left the station to ask for backup and collect the information from Madge about the man who owned the house. They needed anyone she could find: the other deputies, state police, even the chief who would need to be called in from vacation. Dylan didn't know what he was walking into, so he wanted help, but he could not wait for them. He needed to see the display of pictures for himself and most of all, he wanted to see if Autumn was there.

He should have interviewed the kid earlier in the day. If he hadn't been so tired he would have handled the whole situation differently. He said there were a lot of pictures of Autumn 'doing regular stuff.' Someone must have been stalking her for some time and they had professional equipment—a photographic drone if the boy wasn't exaggerating. He had a bad feeling about the whole situation.

If he hadn't had his head in a bottle maybe he would have paid more attention to the warning signals. Instead of laughing at Autumn's concerns, he should have taken them more seriously from the very beginning. He just hoped he wasn't too late. He pressed harder on the accelerator as self-directed anger consumed his thoughts.

The house he was headed for was directly across the lake from Autumn and would be the perfect place for some nut job to stalk her. *Hell,* he could probably see her from the house without a drone but with some simple binoculars or that telescope the kid talked about. What if the psycho snatched Autumn yesterday? That would mean she was under his control for almost two whole days. Dylan felt sweat trickle down his back and he wiped a film of moisture from his forehead. It was likely this was the same guy who caused the disruption at Jan Millers house and took Sadie. As he remembered the dog was covered in blood and had her muzzle taped, he thought *Oh, God,* and he groaned. *How long did he have Jan Miller before Sadie got covered in blood and dumped?*

Wilson shot him a questioning look, then turned back toward the narrow road as they sped around a corner. He ignored her as his thoughts kept escalating. He leaned into the steering wheel and tried to concentrate on the sharp curves. *If he was lucky Autumn might be there. If he was very lucky, she might even be alive.*

As Dylan rounded a corner he felt the car tilt and they almost went onto two wheels, so he eased his foot off the gas. Judy looked at him again and grinned as she said, "Hey, I love me some speed, but let's keep this bad boy on the road, okay?" It was the first time he felt a little fear seeping through the tough exterior. He refused to look at her and engage, so he gripped the steering wheel tighter and bent forward even more as he eased back down on the gas pedal and watched the odometer climb once again.

If they were in Chicago he could have gotten the department to locate Autumn's cell phone—if she still had it with her. Modern technology was one of the other benefits of a larger police department budget. Here, all he could do was keep calling her cell and probably have the crazy on the other end laugh at his increasingly desperate pleas. He almost shouted stop at his thoughts, but instead glanced at Wilson and said, "Call Lucy again and tell her we are almost there and see if she has reached anyone for backup." He grimaced, then added, "Please."

She nodded her head and made the call, but after listening to her terse conversation, she looked at him and shook her head no, and then she slipped the strap on her gun loose.

Dylan nodded back and stared ahead as the headlights lit up the narrow road. A deer at the side of the road lifted its head and stared at the approaching vehicle as headlights reflected in its eyes. He slowed and swerved, but the animal turned and ran back into the woods with a flash of its white backed tail. "Damn," Judy said as she placed her hand on the dashboard.

As he picked up speed again he finally saw the big white house half way down the block. He surged forward and then screeched to a stop in front of the house as his seat belt dug into his shoulder. Dylan cut the engine but left the lights on. After the wild ride the night seemed eerily quiet. Both he and Wilson leaned forward and gazed at the turn of the century mansion. *God, it looks like something out of a Stephen King novel,* he thought. Everything was dark and quiet. The only movement was their revolving colored lights as they painted the white house red and blue.

Dylan jumped out of the car and pulled his gun. He moved around the vehicle toward the house. Wilson was already out of the car and following him, but he paused and held up one hand to stop her and said, "Stay with the car and watch for backup or anyone trying to leave by the front door. But be careful, Autumn Brennan and Jan Miller are still missing, so there could be hostages."

Wilson said in a fierce whisper, "You can't go around there alone, you need me to have your six."

Dylan glared at her and said, "Wilson, for God's sake just say you have my back. Don't use some stupid cop tv jargon. I will be fine, but I don't want this son-of-a-bitch getting away." A glance at the house, then back to her as he continued with, "Besides, there may be more than one and they could scatter." He tried to contain his anger and not direct it at this green cop, "That's an order, Wilson, and stay alert and safe. No heroics."

She blushed bright red and nodded at him, but remained by the car, so he must have gotten through to her. But as she turned toward the house she aimed her gun at the front door. *Geeze, I hope she doesn't shoot some innocent civilian, he thought but kept going.*

He did not want her with him to muck things up and the boys said the display was at the bottom basement level, so that was where he was heading. He had a warrant in hand, so if he happened to come across the jerk responsible for all this, well, then he could release some of his pent-up anger and it would all be legal.

***

Autumn raced through the outer room with only a single glance at Rowen still lying next to the dining room table. Some section of her brain registered that blood soaked one side of his blond head and that it was cushioned in a puddle of red on the floor. She headed straight for the dark hallway and didn't stop until she reached the room next to hers. She stood for a moment in front of the door and then slid the lock back and pulled it open.

The room was a mirror image of her cell. Same small iron bed, little bedside table with a lamp, and sink in the corner, but this room smelled much worse than hers and she could see the source was a half full camp toilet by the sink. She gagged but the image that gripped her heart was the woman lying on the cot.

Autumn felt a chill as she gazed at her in the soft lamplight. She was lying on her back with her eyes closed and looked like a porcelain doll. Her eyes traveled from the woman's braded auburn locks down to the chain encircling her pale ankle. It was not Jan Miller, but she held an even more striking resemblance to Autumn than Jan. It was like some weird dream where she was looking at her dead self.

Rowen was probably telling the truth about killing Jan, Autumn thought as she remembered all the blood on Sadie's fur. This woman was yet another victim of his insane obsession with their mother. *How many?* she thought as moisture filled her eyes.

A deeper chill gripped her heart as she realized she was thinking of him as her brother, but if he was telling the truth about Jan, he could be telling her the truth about her own past. Somehow, she knew his words were true from the beginning. What else could explain her strange dreams? She shook her head. Even though her heart felt it was true, she needed more proof that this monster was related to her before she accepted his words.

Autumn eased into the room and approached the woman. She lay so still that Autumn was afraid she really was dead. There was no sign of breathing and her face was as white as the sheet she lay on. Her clothing was that of a 70's hippy, much like what Autumn was wearing. The blue sequined mini dress against her pale skin made her look even more pitiful. She was barefooted and the skin around her chained ankle was red and bruised, and a pair of platform heels lay on the floor. Strangely, the shoes had glittery lights imbedded in the heels and one of them was flashing as it lay on the concrete floor. It made the whole image even more surreal.

There were dark bruises on the woman's arms, legs, and *oh, god,* around her neck. *What did he do to you?* Autumn thought as a tear spilled over and ran down her cheek. She choked back a sob and swiped the tear away as she felt a hot ball of fire forming in her stomach. She clinched her fists and thought, *No more.*

A quick glance at the door before Autumn leaned over the woman and touched her on the shoulder. At first there was no reaction from the prone woman, but then there was a slight flutter of her eyelids and finally, her eyes opened.

She is alive, Autumn thought, but the pain and fear she saw pooled in those green eyes was almost unbearable, and Autumn took an involuntary step back. Without turning her head, the woman's eyes widened when she saw Autumn in the dim lamp light. Her cracked lips opened, and she tried to speak, but the only sound that came out was a low moan.

Autumn moved forward again and placed her finger to her own lips to signal her to be silent. Rowen was down, but she wasn't certain for how long, so she didn't want to draw him here if he was up. She reached for the bottle of water on the bedside table and held it to the woman's dry lips. She managed to drink a few sips before choking and sputtering, so Autumn put the bottle back and bent close to her ear and whispered, "Can you walk?"

She responded with a tight nod. Doubt and panic replaced the pain Autumn saw in her eyes, but the hand that griped Autumn's wrist was surprisingly strong as the woman said, "I can do it; please don't leave me."

Autumn encircled her shoulders and helped her sit up as she whispered, "I won't leave you; I promise. We are getting out of here together." Once the woman was sitting with her legs over the side of the bed and her bare feet planted on the floor, Autumn bent to examine the lock.

The combination was an eight-letter code instead of numbers just like the one that enslaved Autumn. As she examined the lock she frowned as she ran possible words through her head. *How can I solve this? It's impossible!* There was simply too many possibilities and she felt panic well up and cloud her thoughts. She only had the first letter, 'M,' and that was assuming he used the same code on both her lock and this one.

She stole a quick glance at the woman who was barely maintaining a sitting position. Autumn tried to smile, but the motion felt empty and strained. The look she gave Autumn was somewhere between hope and acceptance. "My name is Erin Watson," she said in a hoarse whisper.

Autumn's stomach twisted. *She wants me to know who she is if she doesn't make it,* Autumn thought. She was not going to leave her. *This woman will not die alone in this horrid room.* Autumn promised not to leave without her, and she did not want to stay, so she shook her head and tried to clear her thoughts. "I am Autumn Brennan and we are getting free," she said to her in a firm voice.

For fun she did a lot of escape rooms with Christina, who was her best friend in Nashville, at least until Chris married and moved across the country. They were a good team at solving puzzles, finding clues, and Autumn excelled at opening locks; all kinds of locks. They did multiple escape rooms, and she usually enjoyed figuring out how the locks worked and what clues went with them.

She loved hearing the click as she succeeded yet again, but there was so much more at stake now than simply getting into the next room before the timer ran out. This was a life or death moment and the pressure was clouding her ability to come up with solutions. *Mother? No, not enough letters, besides, he hated her,* she thought.

Think, Autumn, think, but her thoughts were jumbled, and it was difficult to concentrate. She took a deep breath and let it out. As she bent over the combination lock she cleared her head of what could be and tried to keep it only on what was now. She did the same thing with her performances. Of course, when she was on stage there wasn't a maniac waiting in the wings to burst forward.

Maybe it was the deep breaths, or maybe it was taking herself out of the problem by thinking of performing, but it hit her like a bolt and it fit with the right number of letters. *Michelle.* With trembling fingers, she turned the letters until they lined up: M-I-C-H-E-L-L-E. click. Erin was free. *We are free,* she thought.

It was all Autumn could do to keep from yelping and clapping. She got it on the first try, but there was no winner's board for her name to be posted, only freedom, and that was the best prize she could have asked for.

Autumn stood and helped the battered woman get up from the cot as she placed an arm around her waist. Erin stood and wrapped her arm around Autumns shoulders. They made eye contact and both nodded and smiled before they started moving toward the door.

The trip down the hallway felt as if they were walking on a sandy beach. Each step took a tremendous amount of effort and strength. When they finally reached the main room, Autumn's head swiveled toward the dining room table. A sharp intake of breath. There was a small pool of blood on the floor, but no body.

No Rowen.

Autumn froze and the woman she supported felt it and stiffened as she sensed the danger. Autumn scanned the room in the dim light looking for him, but she could not see his lurking form in the shadows. Her eyes were drawn to the outside door. It still stood open and the curtains gently moved in the evening breeze.

Did he think she ran outside and he followed to look for her, or did he figure it out and was waiting outside to grab them at their first taste of freedom? But, that didn't make sense because he wouldn't chance someone witnessing them from across the lake. *Or would he get off on the danger?* she thought. She remembered how he was hiding behind the door as she first entered the basement and sprang forward. Hide and watch was his specialty.

She felt sweat break out on her forehead as she debated leaving the house or finding a place inside to hide. *What to do?* It was possible he was searching the woods and road and they could avoid him by going in the opposite direction toward the beach, but if he was on the patio, she didn't stand a chance trying to limp away with her injured companion.

"Let me get you hidden and I will check it out," Autumn whispered.

The woman shook her head and her eyes brimmed with fear. She swallowed hard and then whispered in a voice that broke and stumbled over the simple words, "No, please..." then Autumn felt the woman's shoulders stiffen and she mumbled, "Okay, that wasn't fair, you're right," and then her shoulders slumped as she turned her head and gazed back down the hallway with the cells.

Autumn handed her hope and she couldn't take it away. She understood the feeling of desperately wanting out of here and she wouldn't deny this woman the same freedom. "All right, but we may have to move as quickly and quietly as we can out there," Autumn said. A tight nod from Erin and she put her foot forward and grimaced as she attempted a more forceful step.

At the door, Autumn paused and stuck her head out and searched for Rowen. It was dark, but the moon was bright and reflected off the surface of the lake and lit the yard and woods with a soft glow. *Great, now the cloud cover and fog lifts*, she thought, then she froze.

He was there. At the edge of the trees. All six foot something of spindly arms and legs.

His back was to them and he stared toward the woods, then up toward the road. Autumn took a step back into the house and took another deep breath. They stood motionless and Autumn mentally counted to ten, then edged her head through the door again. He was gone.

Autumn swiveled her head around but could see no sign of him. She looked at Erin and nodded and whispered, "We have to try it. I left a kayak on the beach by the lake and we can use that." The woman nodded back, and Autumn guided her out of the door and headed straight for the lake.

As they eased down the hill as fast and as they could manage, Autumn prayed silently that he was still on the road. The moon bathed them in light and she felt completely exposed. Erin stumbled and almost went down, but Autumn managed to catch her and get her upright again.

This woman was in bad shape and Autumn knew she wouldn't be able to go much further, so it was good she had chosen the water instead of walking her out of the area, especially since they were bare footed. Walking without shoes on the grass was one thing, but on the asphalt road, it would be a disaster, and Rowen was persistent, he would keep searching until he found them.

Once they reached the beach, Autumn didn't stop until they were at the kayak. She looked at Erin and asked, "Can you step into it, so I can lower you?" A quick nod and she hiked her tight skirt up even higher as she managed to get one foot over the side and lean into the kayak. Autumn used all her strength to ease her down onto the seat, then she lifted the woman's other foot and put it in as well. She slipped the life vest over her arms and handed her the paddle. "I am going to push you out and you do whatever you can to get across the lake. My house is that one," she said as she pointed in that direction.

"What about you?" Erin asked.

"I'll be okay. There are two more kayaks by the dock and a canoe right here. You just go and don't look back," Autumn said, then added, "No matter what you hear."

Another nod and Erin grabbed Autumn's wrist in a tight grip as she whispered, "Thank you." Autumn gave her a quick hug, then pushed the kayak off the beach until it was all the way into the water, then she waded out and pushed her even harder. The kayak glided across the water and Autumn stood knee deep in the lake and smiled. The sight of the injured woman as she floated away made Autumn feel elated.

"Why did you do that, Michelle?" Autumn stiffened, and the smile slid from her face. The voice coming from behind her was tight and low with anger.

Autumn turned around slowly. Rowen stood at the edge of the sand and glared at her. The side of his head was covered with dried blood, but a little was still oozing from the wound and it dribbled down his cheek. Autumn noticed that he swayed slightly, then corrected and stood tall with his fists clinched by his side. He looked like a petulant child.

He was close. With those long legs he could reach her with one leap. She edged back a step and the water was now swirling around her thighs. It felt cool through the bell bottom jeans and she could feel the mud on the bottom of the lake squishing between her bare toes.

"You should not have freed her; she was mine. You are ruining everything," he growled. "You were supposed to make it better."

"Rowen, you are sick, you know that, don't you?" She eased back another step. Autumn was a very good swimmer and the water was dark enough that she knew he wouldn't be able to see her after the first plunge, but she needed to give Erin a little more time to get farther out on the lake.

"I'm not sick; I'm broken. Mother saw to that. You were always so damn strong. You should have stayed, and I should have been the one to go. I could have done so much with my IQ, but I couldn't stand up to her. You always did." He glared at her and screamed, "You never showed fear, not once."

"I can get you help if you let me," she said. Another step back. She felt a mud hole and edged sideways. "I'm sorry, but that was so long ago, and it wasn't my fault. I had no control over her giving me away. You must know that. I can be there for you now even if I could not be there for you then. I can get you a doctor who could help, plus you are injured, and you probably need stitches. I'm sorry I had to hurt you, but you left me no choice." A car screech sounded from the road somewhere beyond the house. They both glanced in that direction and saw red and blue lights flashing from the front of the house.

Rowen looked back at her shrugged, and said, "I can't be fixed. I will always do what I do, and besides, I like it. It makes life interesting. I would not like being locked up with nothing to do. It would be endlessly boring. I need to play the game." He took a step forward and held out a hand to her as he said, "Come with me. We can be together again. We're twins, we are supposed to be together and support each other. I don't want to be alone anymore."

She watched him as he approached, then glanced over her shoulder. The kayak was barely visible. It had to be closer to the other side than to them. She looked back at Rowen, smiled, and then said, "Sorry." She turned and dove into the water and felt herself surge through the cold darkness.

Autumn swam underwater expecting a grab on her ankle at any moment, but it didn't come. She swam through the dark murky water until her lungs felt as if they would burst. When the need for air over came the desire to be hidden, she barely broke the surface with her head and swam in place as she turned and stared at the beach. It was empty, but she could see Rowen running up the hill toward the big white house. She was far enough away that he looked like a stick figure running man. Red and blue lights were still flashing through the sky over the roof of the house. *Dylan,* she thought.

Autumn hesitated but turned and kept swimming toward her own dock. She could not make herself go back. *Not now.* She wanted home and besides, Erin still needed her help. She swam as hard as she could toward the kayak. She could barely see it, but it looked like it was already at her dock. She pushed forward and felt freer with each kick as she navigated through the inky water.

Chapter 23

Dylan held his gun by his side as he used a pen flashlight to scramble down the hill by the house without falling. When he reached the back patio he stopped, turned off the flashlight and pocketed it before he took a step onto the concrete slab. *What the hell?* he thought. He raised his gun chest high and pointed it toward the window.

Lights blazed from the downstairs basement. The curtains were drawn wide open and there was a tall, thin man standing just inside. The lights backlite him as wild eyes stared back at Dylan. Dylan raised his gun even higher and pointed it at him as he shouted, "Police, hold up your hands."

The man grinned and raised his hands, but something small and black was in the right one. The side of his head was covered in blood as if he had been in a fight, but Dylan couldn't see anyone else in the room. *Where is she?* Dylan thought as he squinted at the object in the man's hand but couldn't tell what it was. *Knife? Small gun?*

Dylan didn't want to shoot him until he found out if he had Autumn, and if so, where he had her. What if she was secreted away somewhere or even at another location? He looked over the man's shoulder searching the room, then he looked back at the man and shouted, "Drop it or I will shoot," but the tall man just laughed and then squeezed the hand with the black object.

Dylan felt the explosion before he heard it, then the force threw him back through the air and the world went silent. As he hit the ground, all he could think was, *Autumn. Was Autumn in the room?* Then everything went black.

***

Autumn heard the explosion as she was helping Erin move up the hill in her yard and she swiveled around toward the lake. An enormous puff of gray smoke shot up from the back of the white house, then settled back down and she could see fire licking at the sky.

Autumn felt a chill and her chest tighten as she heard a shout that sounded like a woman's voice as it carried across the water. She was too far away to hear what she was shouting, but she could have sworn it sounded like "*McAlister?*"

"What happened?" Erin whispered.

"I'm not sure," Autumn mumbled. *Dylan?* she wondered as she bit her lip. She stood and stared at what looked like a video on the evening news instead of a sight from her backyard. She heard footfalls and a bark, so she turned to see Pat and Terri running down her driveway with Sadie on a leash beside them.

"Autumn, thank God! Are you, all right?" Pat shouted as they reached them. She was out of breath, so it came out in a rush.

"We've been so worried about you," Terri added, then looked across the lake and asked, "What on earth happened?"

"I'm not sure, but I think there was an explosion at the white house. Long story, but we were being held there and this woman, Erin Watson, is injured and needs an ambulance." She looked back across the water and said, "Dylan may be at the explosion sight. Do either of you have your cell phones?" Her words felt like they were tumbling out of her and although she wasn't the one who had ran down a hill, she couldn't seem to catch her breath.

"I do," Terri said as she pulled out her phone and called 911. She started telling the operator what happened and asked for an ambulance and fire department to respond. She was gesturing wildly with her free hand as she spoke and added, "Send an ambulance to my house and to the old Miller place as well. We have an injured woman who needs attention here, but there may also be injured at the explosion site."

Pat moved forward and put her arm around Erin's waist and said, "Can you walk a little further? Let's get you to our house and see if we can make you more comfortable while we are waiting. We are veterinary doctors, but maybe we can help."

"It might be better if you bring your car down and drive her over. She is having some trouble walking," Autumn said.

"Good idea," Pat said.

"I'll get it," Terri added as she pocketed her phone and sprinted up the hill.

Pat watched her partner a moment and said, "Damn she is in good shape. I have to work out more." She took Erin from Autumn and began a slow turn toward the hill leading to the driveway.

"Thank you," Autumn said and managed a smile and then turned and again stared across the lake.

With Erin's weight supported by Pat, Autumn suddenly felt so light she feared she would float away, or at the least, fall flat on the ground, but Sadie moved to her side, licked her hand and rubbed against her leg, and she felt grounded again. Autumn stroked the dogs head and she felt tears began to flow down her cheeks. She turned away from the fire and destruction and headed up the hill as she saw Terri speeding down the driveway toward them.

Chapter 24

Autumn slipped into the hospital room and slid into the chair by the bed. Dylan lay perfectly still. He was tucked into his white sheet and blanket like a big burrito. Autumn guessed the night nurses had bundled him up to keep him still. The doctor told her last night that they had sedated him and to let him wake up on his own, so she went home and caught a few hours of much needed sleep.

There were a lot of tubes and monitors connected to him and Autumn wondered what all the numbers meant. She understood a little of it, but with a history of being incredibly blessed with her own health, she did not have a complete grasp, so the moving monitor readings and occasional dings were a little intimidating.

Her eyes roved back to Dylan and his bruised face. Small cuts from the flying glass covered his left cheek and forehead, but luckily, the glass missed his eyes. Since the back of his hand was also covered with the tiny red slashes, she guessed he instinctively covered them. A big white bandage covered his left ear. Again, he was very lucky he did not lose his hearing since he was so close to the blast radiance.

Her first visit this morning was to Erin Watson's room and she was pleased to see she was already up and walking with only a cane for support. Although she was bruised and battered, it seemed Rowen did not do any permanent damage. At least not physically, and only time would tell if she could get past the ordeal mentally. But Autumn thought the woman would heal just fine. She was grateful Erin was one of Rowen's *strong* women.

Erin appeared cheerful and ready to get home. Under the circumstances, her mental state was amazing. *What she went through was horrifying, and she appeared close to death when I found her; now look at her,* Autumn thought. She was already begging the doctors to release her, so she could get home and back to work. Strangely enough, her biggest worry was about her fish, and if someone fed them while she was gone. Autumn was impressed with the woman's resilience and she was glad it ended like it did for her.

She shivered as she thought of Jan Miller. Erin and Autumn came so close to having the same fate. They could be just two more victims of Rowen and he would still be out there playing his evil game. Even if he claimed to be Autumn's brother, he would have eventually seen through her ruse of cooperation and sent her along the same path as Jan. He was already showing indications of resenting her absence almost as much as his mother's cruelty. She sent a silent prayer up for Jan Miller and all of Rowen's other victims. *At least it is over now.*

Autumn leaned forward and pulled herself out of her musings as she sensed movement from the bed. Dylan stirred, and the burrito began bumping as his limbs pushed against their confines. He went still again, and then his eyes fluttered, then flew open and he scanned the room. As the blue orbs fastened on her he smiled. "Hello," he said in a hoarse whisper, then added, "You're alive."

"Hello, yourself," she replied. She got up and grabbed his water glass and held the straw to his chapped lips. He drank greedily, then choked and coughed. It reminded her of when she found Erin and she started to pull it away, but he shook his head and grabbed at the straw with his lips, then drank some more. "Be careful," she said.

He nodded, then plopped his head back on the pillow and said, "Have I been out long?" He struggled with the burrito blanket and she helped him extract his arms.

"All night and half the next day," she said.

A glance at his burrito wrapped body and he raised his eyebrows as he said, "Everything still intact?"

"Yes, you are very lucky. The firemen and first responders said if you were any closer it wouldn't be such a good outcome." She reached out and touched the bed and nodded toward his white cocoon. "You had a pretty serious concussion and I am guessing you got a little restless last night and they wanted to keep you still."

"I was afraid you were in the house."

"I was, but I got away before the bomb went off. It's a long story, and I will save the details for when you are better, but the short version is that I was stupid enough to investigate the house on my own and he grabbed and imprisoned me." She shook her head and made a circular motion with her fingertip against the side of her forehead before she continued with, "After I escaped, I swam across the lake and had just gotten out of the water when I heard the explosion."

"Do you know who took you?"

"The man may actually be my brother, and he said his name is, uh, *was*, Rowen O'Brian," Autumn replied.

"*What?*" Dylan asked.

"That's what he told me anyway, and it was a pretty convincing story. He had information about my adoption and some of the stuff he said I actually dreamed about, so those dreams could be forgotten memories." She looked down, shook her head, then raised it back up and stared into Dylan's eyes as she said, "If he really was my brother, our DNA would be an interesting match, because he also said we were not just brother and sister, but twins, and get this, we still had different fathers."

"Okay, that's more than a little bizarre and sounds like he was delusional."

"I know, *right?* At first, I thought he was making it up, but it is a real thing. *Superfecundation Twins*. I actually Googled it, but I don't know if it's true about us." She leaned forward and added, "At least if we had different father's, even if we were twins, I would only have our mother's strain of DNA shared with him. The guy was certifiable and admitted how much he enjoyed his game of killing and torturing those women--- I really don't want to be connected to him by blood."

"I don't blame you, but you are nothing like that and it does always go back to *nature vs nurture*. You said you were adopted, so there is that. Did he live, or did they at least find his body to make sure he didn't get away? That was a big explosion and he was holding the detonator and was at ground O."

"They are still gathering pieces of him, so he definitely won't be taking any more victims. I'm not even sure they have enough of him to run DNA and I can get some answers." She looked toward the window and said, "Okay, now that was really cold, but honestly, maybe I don't want to know. Some things are better left as a mystery."

"I can't say I am disappointed that he didn't survive the explosion, but if he really is your brother, I'm sorry you won't be able to get more answers, not just from his DNA, but from him," Dylan said as he pushed himself a little further up on the pillow and winced. He reached up to touch his left ear, but it was swathed in the bandage. He tapped gently at the wrapping and said, "No wonder I can't hear that well."

"The doctor said you should regain your hearing. Your eardrum was a little damaged, but it will heal."

"Good. I am grateful, but even more grateful that you weren't still in the house when he detonated the bomb." He gazed at her and said, "Even though you think you don't want to know if he was your brother, not knowing can sometimes be worse, but I am glad you won't be haunted by him living in some institution and always wondering if he will come looking for you again."

She touched his shoulder and then pulled her hand back to rest it on the railing as she said, "He admitted to me that he is, uh, was, a serial killer, and that he killed Jan Miller so that he could give me her dog. It's unbelievable, but he sounded happy about it. He actually thought I would be grateful. How crazy is that?" She sighed, then nodded and said, "You are right about him being in a mental institution or prison. He said that he wasn't 'fixable,' and didn't want to spend the rest of his life locked up in some high security institution, but he deserved that and more instead of death. I am assuming that's why he had the explosion rigged as an end game. Having control to the last." She frowned and felt heat rising from her chest to face and said, "I don't want to feel all this anger I am feeling, but I can't seem to help it. He was brilliant but damaged. He could have done so much good, but instead he inflicted the pain he felt on innocent victims. What a waste."

"Pretty crazy." Dylan's said as his eyes blinked, then he pushed up on his elbows as he said, "How much of the house was destroyed? Do you think there were any other women inside?" He asked as if it suddenly occurred to him and he wanted to get out of the bed to check, then he added, "Did you hear or see anyone else?"

She smiled and put her hands on his shoulders and eased him flat, then said, "You need to rest. The doctor said it was the best therapy. You may experience headaches, some memory loss, nausea—You need to take it easy for a few days and stop trying to save everyone." She sat in the chair again and said, "There was only one other woman, but I got her out when I escaped. Her name is Erin Watson."

"Really? Is she okay?" He asked without turning his head toward her.

"She was in pretty bad shape, but the doctors think she will be all right. In fact, I visited her this morning and she was already up and walking and wants them to release her." A grin and she continued with, "She will probably need to stay a while longer to make sure she is okay, but her spirit is amazing considering what she went through." Autumn leaned forward, and her smile disappeared as she said, "She met him on a dating site. It seems to be how he found his victims and they all resemble me as much as Jan Miller did, but he said I look exactly like *our* mother. It was eerie seeing her and those pictures on the wall full of women who resemble me."

"That makes sense. Easy to create a hunting ground with a computer site complete with pictures and profiles." He closed his eyes, then they flew open and he turned his head toward her and grimaced as he said, "The pictures. The boys told me about them; that's why I was heading to the house in the first place," he touched his head as if the memory just popped into his mind.

Autumn knew things might be fuzzy for him because of the concussion and the doctor said talking about it would be good, so she said, "Yes, that's right. You and Officer Wilson, and she is unharmed by the way. She is the one who got to you first and pulled you away from the fire." He nodded and smiled, and she continued with, "I think he picked his victims and was obsessed with me because he hated our mother. He made us dress up in 70's hippie garb and I have a creepy feeling it might be some of my mother's actual clothing. I hate that I am thinking of her as my mother. I had a wonderful mother and father and I want no part of this looney, dysfunctional family."

"We can't always choose our birth parents, but we can make new families," he mumbled, and then his eyelids fluttered, closed, then popped open again.

"Are you okay?" she asked.

"Yes, please, continue. I want to know everything."

She smiled and said, "Maybe not everything right now, but eventually."

"Well, a little more, now please," he said.

"Okay, okay. I believe the clothing was a big part of his thing, or I guess you would say, ritual. I am guessing it had to do with how much he hated the woman who was his, and possibly my, mother. If he was telling the truth, it appears I came from some very questionable lineage. Not just our DNA, but our mother seemed to be quite cruel, also."

A nurse entered the room and said, "You're awake." She moved to the equipment and checked all the mysterious numbers and monitors, then patted Dylan on the shoulder and said, "I'll go get your doctor."

Autumn stood and said, "I had better go also and let you get some more rest. I will take care of Sadie and then come back later to see how you are doing. Thanks for taking care of her by the way."

"No problem. Sorry about the kitchen window," he said as the nurse moved to the other side of the bed and tucked his burrito sheet in even tighter, but she allowed his arms to stay free. She held his wrist and checked his pulse.

Autumn laughed and said, "I'm not. Poor Sadie must have been desperate for someone to come to her rescue, and Ying and Yang will probably not forgive me for a while." She stood and touched his other arm and said, "Can I bring you anything?"

"Maybe a change of clothes. I imagine the ones I was wearing might be a little worse for wear. Oh, and if you have time, could you feed and walk Ollie?"

"Sure, maybe I'll introduce Sadie to him and take them both for a walk. I can keep him overnight if they get along as long as it's okay with you." She adjusted her smile into a straight line and added, "Where are your keys? I don't want to break a window to get in."

An eye roll, then he said, "The keys were in my pocket before the explosion. Of, course, he can stay with your menagerie, and I can't imagine him not fitting in; he loves everyone and every fur creature. I bet he will even love your shadowy cats." He shifted in the bed and grimaced as the nurse dropped his arm and moved back to the equipment and adjusted his IV. "My head is starting to hurt again," he said to her.

The nurse nodded toward the cupboard in the corner then said to Autumn, "His clothes are in there," before she turned to Dylan and said, "I'll see if I can get you something for that," then left the room. She wasn't the friendliest of the hospital staff, but she seemed to be taking good care of him. Most of the doctors and nurses Autumn interacted with at the hospital were more than kind, but you never knew what was going on inside someone or what battles they were fighting.

"My cats aren't 'shadowy,' they are simply careful and discriminate."

"Right." He said and closed his eyes again.

Autumn slipped around the bed and found his soiled clothing tucked into a big plastic hospital bag. She fished through the bag, and then reached gingerly into his pants pocket. An odd smell of spent gunpowder floated out of the bag as the clothing shifted position. She recognized that smell.

She went by the explosion site earlier in the morning to view the damage. It was horrific, and the same smell hung in the air. After viewing the damage, she decided Dylan was indeed lucky the entire deck had not collapsed on him.

The glass windows and door of the basement were gone, and Autumn did not want to think about which body parts of her captor clung to the shredded curtain and rubble as the forensic team picked at the items and placed them in evidence bags. The team was sweeping the entire area and it was cordoned off with bright yellow crime scene tape. They sent her away, but the scene was burned into her memory, as was the smell. It must be what so many have experienced in foreign lands. It made her feel blessed to live somewhere that it wasn't a common occurrence.

She held up the keys and shook them after she raised up from the bag. He smiled, and then his eyes fluttered closed again. Autumn wondered if the nurse had adjusted a sedative into the IV she was working on. It was just as well. He needed the rest.

As she turned to go, an impulse pulled her back to Dylan and she gave him a peck on the forehead. Her steps felt light as she headed from the room and toward the elevator at the end of the hallway.

***

Autumn pulled her truck in front of the big white house and parked. She leaned forward and gazed at the rambling old house and couldn't help but admire its vintage beauty despite the scenes that played out in her head every time she came here. She wondered if anyone would ever want to live in it again with its history. Perhaps the home saw tragedy before and survived--- and would again. It wasn't what happened to a house that made it a home, it was who lived there and loved it.

The news vans were long gone, but they would probably be back as soon as the story of the bodies leaked to the press. *Bodies not body.* Apparently, Jan Miller had a lot of company. Autumn sighed and got out of the truck and headed around the house toward the water.

The back of the house was still covered in crime scene tape but the section where the explosion happened had yellow plywood panels nailed over the blown-out windows and door. It looked like someone was trying to create a Halloween haunted house, but these frights were real. *I wonder if it's going to become the place where kids whisper and dare each other to approach it on Halloween?* Autumn thought. She could only imagine how those poor women suffered before they found an escape at Rowen's hands.

She stood at the top of the yard and turned her gaze toward the lake. There was a large boat floating almost at the end of the inlet toward the deep part of the lake. She could see one diver's head bobbing in the water and another standing in the boat with a couple of uniformed officers. Two coroner's vans were parked in the yard at the water's edge, along with several branches of law enforcement. Autumn heard they called in the state police and the FBI as well. She gazed beyond them to her house on the other side of the lake. She left her curtains open and she could just make out Sadie's head in the window. A beacon of calm in the tragic events playing out before her.

A grim Officer Wilson was standing by five black body bags stretched out on the grass not far from the sandy beach. She was writing something on a clipboard, and from the set of her mouth and slope of her shoulders, her usual exuberance was missing. She was like a balloon that someone pricked with a pin. It was a shame, but maybe now she would look at tragic crime a little differently. Dylan gave a detailed description of her attitude to Autumn on the night they spent so much time talking. It was a horrible way to learn, but perhaps experiencing this tragedy, she would no longer look at these kinds of crimes as an opportunity to try out her cop chops.

Autumn spotted Dylan and began to move toward him. He was standing on the dock and shouting something to the men in the boat. As she moved forward he turned and saw her. They made eye contact and he waved, then held up a hand for her to stop and began moving toward her.

Autumn closed the distance between them and as she reached him he said, "Hi, let's go back up to the house. You really don't want to see it if they bring up another one. Some of them have been in the water a long time and are in pretty bad shape."

She nodded and turned and moved with him back up the hill and around the house toward her truck. When they reached the truck, he was grimacing, and his face was flushed, so she turned to him and said, "Are you all right? How is your leg? I noticed you were limping. Do you need to stay, or would you like a ride back to your house or the station?"

"I'm okay and I better stay, at least for a while," he said, then pulled a pill bottle from his pocket and downed a little white pill before he added, "The leg is fine, just a little tight and sore; it's the headaches that are tough, but the doc said they would improve soon. At least they took the bandage off my ear, so I don't look like the walking wounded. I haven't regained all my hearing in that ear, but it's better." He turned toward the house and said, "They've covered this end of the lake, so I hope that's it, but he was placing them in the water from his boat, so there could be more in the deeper part of the lake." Dylan ran his hand through his hair and dropped his head as he said, "He weighed them down with a chain from their ankles attached to a concrete cinder block. The divers are used to seeing a body floating underwater, but this freaked them out. It was like an underwater graveyard."

Autumn leaned her head back and closed her eyes a moment as she pictured herself silently floating in the dark cold water with the other women nearby. She realized that she probably swam past them on the night of her escape. She shook her head and said, "Horrible. I wish there was some way I could have known and stopped him."

"I don't believe that was possible, and even if you met him sooner and became aware of what he was doing, you would have simply become an earlier victim."

"I have a gut feeling our mother may have been his first," she mumbled. "Maybe he didn't hurt her in the same way, but I am sure he facilitated her passing."

"Your gut is pretty intuitive since it was you who suggested we try the lake when we were looking for the bodies." He leaned against her truck and said, "We used the cadaver dogs in the woods and by the house and didn't find anything. It's possible we might have given up without your lead."

Autumn gazed at the house and said, "It was what he said about having them near him and the way he was staring at the window in the direction of the water. He said, "Here but not here," and later when he caught up to us on the beach and Erin was drifting away in the kayak he said she was joining *them*. It made me think. I wasn't sure if it was just crazy ramblings from a madman, or some hidden meaning, but he seemed to enjoy being cryptic."

Dylan nodded then said, "Are you more certain you have the same mother? I notice you are referring to her as 'our' mother more. Are you going to research it?"

Autumn looked at Dylan and said, "It has a ring of truth to it, but I don't think I will look into it any further. If she was my mother, and he was my brother, they are both dead, so what would it help to know?"

"Do you want me to check it out for you?"

A smile. "No, that is kind of you, but, at least for now, I want to let it drop. I want to move forward not back. I had wonderful adoptive parents who loved me right up until the end of their lives, perhaps even more because they chose me. That is more than a lot of people can say."

Dylan nodded again and said, "I hear you on that."

She shook her head, then looked at him and said, "Would you like to come to Cowboys on Saturday? I am going to sing." She held up her hands and shrugged at the look of surprise in his eyes and she said, "I know I said I wanted to concentrate on writing my music instead of performing, but I am feeling the need to get back out there around people again."

"I think that's a great idea and I would love to come."

"Good. Pat and Terri are coming, also." She pushed off the truck and said, "Are you sure you don't want a ride home? You look tired and the doc said you should pace yourself."

"No, I'll get one of the guys to drop me off soon, but I might want a ride when you perform, or I would be happy to chauffer."

She laughed and said, "You are welcome to come with me and I will drive. Since you are still on the injured list you will be able to get away with being the one chauffeured for a while." She grinned and said, "It's a date."

Dylan laughed and waved as she got into the truck and turned it around to head home.

Home. It was good to have her home back. She no longer had the feeling of being watched and she didn't think knowing about the women in the lake would ruin it for her. It might give her pause for a while when she looked at the water, but she would offer up a prayer for them and hoped eventually she was only going to see swans and ducks instead of floating bodies. She might even take down the curtains on the picture window in the dining room, or at least leave them open more often.

Autumn read that fear stems from the unknown and felt that it was true. What was that quote? *Ah, yes, "Fear is limiting, and love is limitless."* In a strange way she felt connected to those women and felt lighter knowing they would now be returned to their loved ones.

They are finally free, Autumn thought. Their families will have closure. Maybe burying their loved ones removes the hope that they will come home someday, but it also gives them the ability to grieve and move forward with their lives.

She would like to find out if Jan Miller was being buried and where. Her family told Dylan that Autumn could keep Sadie, but she wanted to take the dog to say goodbye to her companion. It felt right.

Autumn smiled as she drove around a curve in the road. The lake could return to its original beauty and she would give her old house a new life. *This time I'm not running away.* Life was now. Not yesterday or tomorrow, but now. *The hell with Rowen*, she thought. She didn't care if he was her brother or not, but she would not allow him to reach from the grave to control her life in anyway. Her life was hers.

She gazed at the trees as if seeing them for the first time. They were a blaze of fall color and a crisp wind rustled and moved a few leaves across the road. The season was moving forward, and winter was on its way. *I wonder what winter will be like here on the lake,* she thought.

Autumn had a sudden vision of a Christmas tree by a blazing fire and chuckled. *Home,* she thought as she increased her speed and lowered the window to feel the breeze push through her hair.

The End

Made in the USA
Middletown, DE
17 July 2021